Sabine Baring-Gould

Kitty Alone

Vol. 3

Sabine Baring-Gould

Kitty Alone
Vol. 3

ISBN/EAN: 9783337253912

Printed in Europe, USA, Canada, Australia, Japan

Cover: Foto ©Andreas Hilbeck / pixelio.de

More available books at **www.hansebooks.com**

KITTY ALONE

MORRISON AND GIBB, PRINTERS, EDINBURGH

KITTY ALONE

A STORY OF THREE FIRES

BY

S. BARING GOULD

AUTHOR OF

"IN THE ROAR OF THE SEA" "THE QUEEN OF LOVE"
"MEHALAH" "CHEAP JACK ZITA" ETC. ETC.

IN THREE VOLUMES

VOL. III

METHUEN & CO.

36 ESSEX STREET, W.C.

LONDON

1894

CONTENTS OF VOL. III

—⬩—

CHAPTER XXXVII

THE ANSWER OF CAIN

THE accommodation of the little inn was not extensive, so Pasco had to be put into the same room with the lawyer, and Kitty slept with the innkeeper's daughter.

Pasco would have greatly preferred a room to himself. He was in a condition of unrest. As it was not possible for him to return to Coombe Cellars that night, he was in ferment of mind, uncertain whether it were advisable that he should return there that week, whether he should not go with Mr. Squire to Tavistock to make provision for the burial of his uncle, and to see after his estate. He had added crime to crime to save his credit as a man of substance, and all had been in vain. The succession to his uncle's estate supplied him with what he required. Why had not the old man died a day earlier? Why, but that fate had impelled him into crime only then to mock him. If fate could play such malicious tricks with him,

7

might it not pursue its grim joke further, lift the veil, disclose what he had done, and just as the property of his relative came to him, just as the money from the insurance company was due—strike him down, drive him into penal servitude, if not send him to the gallows? He tossed on his bed ; he could not sleep.

At one moment he resolved to go with the solicitor to Tavistock, and remain there till the funeral, or till he received news of what had taken place at home. But a devouring desire to know what had happened, what was the extent of his crime, to know whether Jason had escaped, whether the fire had been put out, what his wife thought, what was the general opinion relative to the fire,—all this drew him homewards.

Moreover, his sprained ankle and arm were painful, and he could lie on one side only. In the night he put out his hand for his coat, drew it to him, and groped for the box of lucifer matches. He desired to light a candle, rise, and bind a wet towel round his foot.

But the box was missing.

Alarmed, he started from bed and explored the pockets of his trousers and of his waistcoat, and then again went through all those of his coat, but in vain. He had lost the box.

Here was fresh cause for uneasiness. Where had he lost it? Surely not at Coombe Cellars. With a sigh of relief, he recalled having struck a light in the linhay in Miller Ash's field, and that it had excited the interest of Kate. He had then slipped it back into his pocket, as he believed.

In all likelihood it had fallen out when he was thrown from the cart on the moor.

Towards morning he dropped into broken sleep, from which he started every few moments in terror, imagining that a constable was laying hold of him, or that he saw Jason Quarm leaping upon him enveloped in flames.

When he woke, he saw the lawyer dressing himself and shaving. His face was lathered about chin and neck and upper lip. He turned towards Pepperill and said, "You are a nice fellow to have as a comrade in a bedroom."

"Am I? Well, I daresay I am," answered Pasco, always prepared for a recognition of his merits.

"I was speaking ironically, man," said Mr. Squire. "By George! how you did toss and tumble in the night. If I had had an uneasy conscience, you would have kept me awake. What was the matter with you?"

"With me? Nothing. I never slept sounder."

"Then you must give your wife bad nights at home. I thought it might have been your spill."

"Oh yes, to be sure it was that. I suffered in my arm and foot; and look, I'm all black and yellow this morning. I shall go back at once to Coombe Cellars."

"You will? Why, man alive, we want you at Tavistock. There is your poor uncle's funeral, you know, to see to. I say, if we are to travel together, you won't cry over-much, will you? I love tears, but in moderation."

"I must return to the Cellars, if only for an hour. I wish to tell Zerah—that's my wife—our piece of good fortune—I mean, our sad bereavement. And I must put together my black clothes and get my hat."

"If it must be, it must. I wish you had been communicated with earlier."

"Earlier? Was that possible?"

"Of course it was; the old gentleman died two days ago."

"Two days ago? Why, to-day is Wednesday."

"Well, his decease took place at five in the morning of Monday."

"Why did you not tell me at once?" almost shrieked Pasco, swinging from his bed, and then collapsing on his crippled foot.

"Bless you, man, it was not my place to do so. I knew nothing of you; the housekeeper was the person he trusted. I came to know of it, as I managed your uncle's affairs. When I inquired about relatives, then I heard of you, or rather got your address, and came off. You see, as he died on Monday, it won't do for you to be away long. The housekeeper has instructions, and is a sensible woman, but you are the proper person to be on the spot."

"Is she honest? Will she make away with things?"

Mr. Squire shrugged his shoulders.

"I will run to Coombe; we will go in the chaise, and return to Tavistock directly I have been there. Kitty shall be driven by the boy to Brimpts in my trap."

Pasco would not have his niece at Coombe for some time if he could help it.

As soon as he was dressed he was impatient to be off.

He hurried breakfast, and hardly ate anything himself. He gave instructions that Kate was to be sent on at once, and was not content till he had seen her off. He had not deemed it prudent to warn her again not to speak of his return to the Cellars after leaving Coombe. To do so might excite her suspicions. Besides, she would be at Brimpts, where there was no one interested in the affairs of Coombe —no one who belonged to it. It would suffice to caution her when she came back to the Cellars, and that return he would delay on one excuse or another.

When Pasco seated himself in the chaise beside the solicitor, an expression of satisfaction came over his face. He was returning to Coombe as a man of consequence, and in good society. How the villagers would stare to see him in a carriage drawn by post-horses. An April weather reigned in his heart, now darkening with apprehension, then brightening with pride and self-satisfaction.

Ever and anon the ghastly figure of his brother-in-law in the sack, burning, rose before his mind's eye, but he put it from him.

As the chaise entered Ashburton, Pepperill said to his companion—"Will you accommodate me with a sum of money till I come in for my inheritance?"

"With the greatest pleasure, but I have not much loose cash about me."

"You have your cheque-book. The circumstances are these—I owe money for wool to a fellow named Coaker, and gave him a bill—unfortunately, I could not meet it, the bank returned it, only a few days ago, and this has made

me very angry. I should like to show the bank and Coaker
that I am not the moneyless chap that they choose to
consider me."

"I shall be happy to assist you. Let us go to the bank
at once; I'll settle that little matter with them. Shall I do
it for you?"

"I shall be obliged, but I think I must go also."

It was possible that the tidings of what had taken place
might have reached Ashburton—possible, though hardly
probable.

His uneasiness was relieved when he entered the bank.
No allusion was made to any fire. The banker was profuse
in his apologies. He could not help himself. There were
certain rules in his affairs that he was bound to follow. He
had no doubt it was an oversight of Mr. Pepperill not to
pay in the sum required, but a man so full of business as
he was reputed to be was liable to such slips of memory.
The banker knew Mr. Squire by reputation, was quite sure
all was as it should be. He would at once communicate
with Coaker—indeed, Coaker was sure to be in Ashburton
that day, and let him have the money of the bill.

For some distance Pasco held up his head, and talked
boastfully. He had taught that banker what he really was.
Everyone else knew he was a man of his word and a man
of substance. The solicitor was glad of this change in his
companion's mood, and talked chirpily.

But the change in Pepperill's manner did not last long.
As he neared Newton, he leaned back in the carriage. He
did not desire to be recognised and saluted with the news

of the fire. The chaise drew up for the horses to be
watered at the inn which had been rebuilt after a fire.

"Will you have a drop of something?" asked the solicitor.
"I shall descend for a minute. I suppose we have not got
far to go now?"

He left the chaise, and left the door open. Pasco closed
it, and being affected with sneezing, opened his pocket-
handkerchief and buried his face in the napkin, as the
landlord came to the door.

He did not lower the kerchief, he listened from behind
it to the host conversing with Mr. Squire.

"Fine morning, sir—come from far?"

"No, nothing very great to-day. Off the moor and
through Ashburton."

"Going on to Teignmouth, sir?"

"No, only to a place called Coombe."

"Coombe-in-Teignhead? You haven't many miles
more. Nice place. Just heard there has been a fire there."

"Indeed. Insured?"

"Can't say, sir. My little place was burnt down. A
tramp slept in the tallat over the pigs and set it ablaze with
his pipe. Happily, I was insured, and now I have a very
respectable house over my head. What will you please to
take, sir?"

"Some rum and milk, I think."

Then Mr. Squire and the landlord went within, and
Pasco lowered his kerchief. He wished he had heard more
—that the man had entered into particulars, and yet he
dared not inquire.

Presently the lawyer stepped into the carriage. The host attended him, and in shutting the door, caught sight of Pasco.

"Halloo!" he exclaimed. "Mr. Pepperill, have you heard the news?"

"News—what news?"

"Why, rather bad for you. There's been a terrible fire at your place."

"The house?"

"I really don't know particulars. They say it's been dreadful. I'm sorry to have to say it, but I hope there's no lives lost, and that you are insured."

"Drive on!" shouted Pasco to the postilion. "Drive on—lose no time. There is a fire at my house."

The horses whirled away, and Pasco no longer disguised his nervousness. It was natural that he should be uneasy.

"You needn't trouble yourself," said Mr. Squire. "If lives had been lost you would have heard, and if you are insured to full value, well"—

On reaching the summit of the hill whence Coombe was visible, a sickly scented smoke was wafted into the carriage windows.

"By George, I can smell it!" exclaimed the solicitor. "It is a sort of concentrated essence of burnt wool."

"Then my stores are gone!" cried Pepperill. "And all the fleeces for which I have just borrowed two hundred pounds of you to pay—all lost. I'm a ruined man."

"Not a bit," answered the lawyer. "You are insured."

The postilion needed no urging; he cracked his whip,

and the horses flew down hill, the chaise rattled through the village, past the church and the inn, whence the host came out to see whether a distinguished guest was coming, and drew up at the entrance to the paddock before the Cellars.

A crowd of villagers, men, women, and children, was assembled round the wreck of the storehouse, from which volumes of smoke still ascended. Every now and then stones and bricks exploded, and the children shouted or screamed if a hot cinder flew out and fell near them.

Pasco burst out of the carriage and rushed towards his house, pushed his way through the assembled crowd, and ran to his door.

There stood Zerah, ghastly in her pallor, her usually well-ordered hair dishevelled, with clenched hands held to her breast, a look of despair in her face. Directly she saw her husband, she shrank from him, and when he put out his hands to her, she thrust him away, with an expression of horror.

" I will not be touched by you," she said hoarsely. " Where is Jason ? "

" Jason ? Am I his keeper ? "

" The answer of Cain," retorted Zerah. " This is your doing. I knew it would come, when you insured. And you have destroyed my brother also. O my God ! my God ! Would that I had never seen this day ! "

CHAPTER XXXVIII

P ASCO thrust his wife within and shut the door behind. Zerah had returned early in the morning, and had found that her husband and Kate were away, and the house locked, whilst the stores were in conflagration. Half the parish was present. The fire had broken out some time after nightfall—at least, it had been observed about nine o'clock by a boy connected with the mill, who ran to the alehouse and roused the village orchestra, which was practising there, and in ten minutes nearly everyone in the little place was at the Cellars. The fire was pouring in dense sheets of flame out of the windows. It had apparently begun below, the wool above dropped into it as the rafters and boards gave way. Nothing could be done to arrest it, but precautions were adopted to prevent the fire communicating with a little rick of straw that Pepperill had for litter near the stables. The flames and smoke were carried inland, and no apprehensions were entertained of the house becoming ignited.

Much comment was made on the absence of Pasco, his wife, and niece. But that which excited most uneasiness was the presence of Jason Quarm's cart and donkey in the yard. If they were at the Cellars, then Jason could not be far distant. Was it possible that, finding the house locked up, and his relatives absent, he had made his way into the store-shed and perished there? This was the question hotly debated.

When Mrs. Pepperill arrived from the other side of the river, and saw the conflagration, and heard that there was a probability that her brother had fallen a victim, she was driven frantic with terror and grief. In her mind connecting her husband with the occurrence, she charged him with the firing of the stores and with the death of her brother.

Pepperill endeavoured to pacify her. He protested his innocence; he declared that he had left the house soon after herself, and by entreaty, remonstrance, and threat urged Zerah to hold her tongue and not recklessly put him in peril by rousing against him suspicion which was without grounds.

As to Jason, he knew nothing about him. He had probably left his trap at the Cellars and crossed the water on some business of his own. He would return shortly. The fact of his cart and ass being there was not sufficient to cause alarm for his safety. If anything transpired more grave, Pasco would be the first to take the necessary steps to investigate what had become of him. Meanwhile, let Zerah moderate her transports and listen to the news he had to tell. He must leave her, and that immediately, to go with the lawyer to Tavistock, and make provision for his uncle's interment and for securing his property.

Pepperill was unable to get away as soon as he wished. He was forced to show himself among the crowd, to give expression to consternation, to answer questions as to his surmises about the origin of the fire, to explain how he had left the place before it broke out, and to offer suggestions as to the whereabouts of Quarm. He scouted the idea of his brother-in-law having been burnt in the stores; he said he suspected the fellow Redmore of having set fire to his buildings. Redmore was at large still; he, Pasco, had given him occasion of resentment by sending the workmen at Brimpts in pursuit of him. The man was a bitter hater and revengeful, as was proved by his having burned the stack of Farmer Pooke. What more likely than that he had paid off his grudge against himself—Pepperill—in like manner?

As soon as ever Pasco was able to disengage himself from the crowd, he re-entered the chaise and departed with the lawyer, glad to escape the scene. When the chaise had got outside Coombe, he leaned back with a puff of relief and said, "That is now well over."

"I should hardly say *that*," observed the lawyer, "till you have the insurance money clinking in your pocket. Now look here, Mr. Pepperill; it may be you will have a hitch about the same. If so, apply to me."

Among those looking on upon the mass of glowing, spluttering combustible material was the rector, with his hands behind him, and his hat at the back of his head. He was touched on the arm, and, turning, saw the pretty face of Rose Ash looking entreatingly towards him.

"What is it, my child?"

"Please, sir, do you think anything dreadful has happened to Kitty's father?"

The rector paused before he answered. Then he said leisurely, "I do not know what reply to make. I saw him last night about seven. I was at my garden-gate when he drove by, and we exchanged salutations."

"The neddy is in the stable here, and there is his cart," said Rose.

"He may have crossed the water."

"But, sir, Mrs. Pepperill had the boat."

"True—is there no other?"

"Yes; the old boat. I did not think of that. I'll run and see if her be in place."

Rose left, and returned shortly, discouraged, and said—

"The old boat be moored to the landing-stage as well as the new boat. And, sir, I do not think he could have got across the water after seven by any boat. The tide was out. By nine, when it was flowing, the people were running about here because of the fire."

"I will go and see Mrs. Pepperill."

"May I come with you, sir? Kitty is my very dear friend."

"Kitty?—I thought she had no friends?"

"It is only quite lately we have become friends. I would do anything for her. I am not happy. I think she ought to know what has taken place, and yet I wouldn't frighten and make her miserable without reason. That is why I so much wish to know what is really thought about

poor Mr. Quarm.   It would be too dreadful if he had come
by his end here, and it will break Kitty's heart."

"You shall come with me, certainly, Rose."

On entering the house, they found Mrs. Pepperill moving
restlessly about the kitchen.   Her mood had gone through
a change since the visit of her husband.   The wildness of
her first terror and grief had passed away, and given place
to great nervous unrest.   She had smoothed her hair as
well as she could with her trembling fingers; her lips
quivered, her eye was unsteady, and she could not remain
in one posture or in one place for more than half a minute.

She had hitherto appeared a hard, iron-natured woman
without sympathy, but now the shock had completely
broken her down.   She had rushed to the conclusion that
her husband had deliberately set fire to his warehouse, and
without scruple had sacrificed her brother.   The horror of
the death Jason had undergone, and the greater horror to
her of the thought that this was the callous act of her own
husband, had shaken the woman out of all her self-restraint
and rigidity of nerve.   She was morally as well as physically
broken down.   A woman stern, uncompromising, strictly
honest and upright, harsh and unpitying in her severity,
she found herself involved in a terrible crime that touched
her in the most sensitive part.   It was the conceit mingled
with stupidity in Pasco, his recklessness in speculation, and
his obstinacy in refusing to listen to her voice, which had
hardened and embittered the woman.

Something he had said, something in his manner, had led
her to fear he contemplated an escape from his difficulties

by dishonest means, and it was to avert the necessity of his
having recourse to these that she had produced her little
store, the savings of many years. When she returned from
Teignmouth to find that her husband, notwithstanding, had
carried out his purpose, and in doing so had swept her
own brother out of his path—then all her fortitude gave
way.

After the first paroxysm of resentment and despair had
passed, she felt the need of using self-control, and of con-
cealing what she thought, of endeavouring to avert suspicion
from falling on Pasco. Now also, for the first time in her
life, did this stern woman crave for sympathy, and her
heart turned at once instinctively to the girl she had
disregarded and despised. Dimly she had perceived,
though she had never allowed it to herself, that there was
a something in her niece of a strong, noble, and superior
nature to her own. And in this moment of terrible
prostration of her self-respect and weakness of nerve, her
heart cried out with almost ravenous impatience for Kate.
To Kitty alone could she speak her mind, in Kitty's breast
alone find sympathy.

When, therefore, the door opened and the rector entered
with a girl at his side, her eyes, dazzled by the sunlight
behind them, unable to distinguish at the moment through
the haze of tears that formed and dried in her eyes, she
cried out hoarsely—

"It is Kitty! I want you, Kitty!"

"I am not Kitty," said Rose. "I am only her dear
friend. If you want Kitty, I will fetch her."

"I do want her. I must have her," said Zerah vehemently.
"I have no one. My brother is dead, my husband is gone.
My Kitty—where is she? I do not know if it is true that
she is on the moor. She may be burning yonder, along wi'
her father."

The woman threw herself into the settle, and burst into
a convulsion of tears.

Mr. Fielding spoke words intended to console her. She
must not rush to a conclusion so dreadful without sufficient
cause; it was possible enough that in the course of the day
something might transpire which would give them reason to
believe that Mr. Quarm was safe. Then, to divert her mind
from this point to one less distressing, as he thought, he
inquired whether she had any idea as to how the fire had
originated.

He could hardly have asked a question more calculated
to agitate her. Zerah sprang from the settle, walked
hurriedly about the room, hiding her eyes with her hand,
and crying—

"I know nothing. I cannot think. I want Kitty."

Then Mr. Fielding put forth his arm, stayed her, and
said—

"Mrs. Pepperill, remember, however dear to you your
brother may be, he must be dearer to Kitty, as he is her
father. You are advanced in life, have had your losses and
sorrows, and have acquired a certain power to sustain a loss
and command sorrow, but Kitty's is a fresh young heart,
that has never known the cutting blows to which yours has
been subjected. Spare her what may be unnecessary. Let

us wait over to-day, and if nothing happens to relieve our minds of the terrible fear that clouds them, we will send to Dart-meet for the child. Indeed, she must be brought here —if our fears receive confirmation. All I ask is, spare her what, please God, is an unnecessary agony."

Then Rose Ash came up close to the bewildered woman.

"Mrs. Pepperill, I will go after Kitty, I promise you, if you will wait over to-day. I am Kitty's friend, as I was once the friend of your Wilmot, and if you will suffer me, I will remain in the house with you, to relieve you, all day, and do what work you desire."

"No, no!" gasped Zerah; "I must be alone. I will have no one here but Kitty."

"You consent to the delay?"

The woman did not refuse; she shook herself free from Rose and the rector, retreated to the window, and cast herself on the bench in it, and cried and moaned in her hands held over her face.

When Rose proposed to Mrs. Pepperill that she should go to Brimpts to fetch Kate, a scheme had formed itself in her brain. She would ask Jan Pooke to drive her. At the time of our story two-wheeled conveyances, gigs, buggies, tax-carts, were kept only by the well-to-do, and there were but three in all Coombe—the parson's trap, and those of Pasco Pepperill and yeoman Pooke. Her own father, the miller, though a man of substance, had not taken the step of providing himself with a trap; to have done so would have been esteemed in the parish an assertion of wealth and importance that would have provoked animadversion, and might have hurt his trade. The miller is ever regarded with mistrust. His fist is said to be too much in the meal-sack, and had he dared to start a two-wheeled conveyance, it would at once have been declared that it was maintained, as well as purchased, at the expense of those who sent their corn to be ground at his mill.

But now that Rose considered her scheme at leisure, it did not smile on her as at first. At the moment she proposed it, the prospect of a long drive by Jan's side, of union in sympathy for Kitty, had promised something. Now that she reviewed her plan, she foresaw that it might be disastrous. Kate, when she heard the tidings of the fire and the news of the disappearance of her father, would be thrown into great distress, and a distressed damsel is proverbially irresistible to a swain. It might undo all that Kate had done, make Jan more enamoured than ever, and he as a comforter might gain what he had failed to win when he approached as a lover. Rose was a good-hearted, if a somewhat wayward girl. She desired to do a kind thing to Kitty, but not at such a cost to herself.

She turned the matter over in her head, and finally reached a compromise. She would ask Jan to drive her to Brimpts so as to fetch Kate, but lay the injunction on him, for Kitty's sake, not to say a word relative to the loss of her father. Grieved Kate would be to hear of the burning of the storehouse, but not heart-broken. The consumption of so much coal would not extort tears. A sorrowful girl is only interesting—a heart-broken one is irresistible.

CHAPTER XXXIX

ONE FOR THEE AND TWO FOR ME

ROSE and Jan were side by side in the trap that belonged to the Pookes. In his good-nature and readiness to do whatever was kind, Jan had promptly acceded to Rose's request that he should help her to bring Kitty home. It was not right, she said, that the child should be left on the moor, when her father was dead, and her aunt in despair.

"You know, Jan," she said, pressing against the driver's side, and speaking low and confidentially, "I am dear Kitty's very, very best friend,—I may say, her only real friend,—and have to fight her battles like a Turk."

"I did not know that," observed Jan in surprise, ill-disguised, for his mind ran to the incidents of the Ashburton fair.

"You boys don't know everything. I love Kitty dearly, and I believe she loves me. We have no secrets from each other, and now that she is in trouble, my heart flies out to she, and I want to be with her, and break the news to her very, very gently."

"I thought"—began Jan, then paused.

Rose looked up in his dull, kindly face, and said roguishly, "Oh, Jan, a penny for your thoughts. No, really; I will give half a crown—a thought with you must be *so* precious, because so rare."

A little nettled, Jan said, "I thought this, Rose: from your treatment of Kate the other day at the fair, that you were her enemy rather than her friend."

"That is because you are an old buffle-head. Of course we are bosom friends, but I'm full of fun, and we tease one another—we girls—just as kids gambol. You are so heavy and solemn and dull, you don't understand our gambols. You are like a great ox looking on at kids and lambs, and wondering what it all means when they frisk, and you take it for solemn earnest."

"But about the quarrel at the stall—the kerchief?"

"That was play."

"And the workbox that Noah knocked from under her arm? Was that play?"

"Purely. Jan, I had a much better workbox which I wanted to give Kate, and you went and spoiled my purpose by giving her that trumpery affair. I am not ashamed to own it. I told Noah to strike it from under her arm, that I might give her the box I had put aside for her."

"And she has it?"

"Yes; oh dear, yes!—of course she has it."

Jan shook his head; he was puzzled, but supposed all was right—supposed, because he was too straightforward and good-hearted to mistrust the girl who spoke so frankly,

with great eyes looking him full in the face, and smiling.
Impudence is more convincing than innocence.

Then Rose said, "How good you are, Jan — how
tremendously good! Really, it is a privilege to live in
the same parish, and drive in the same buggy beside so
excellent a Christian."

"What are you at now?" was Jan's outspoken response.

"I mean what I say, Jan. Considering how you've been
treated, I declare that by your conduct you do a lot more
good to me than any number of sermons."

"How so? You are making game of me."

"Not a bit; I'm serious. How is it you show your goodness? Why, by driving me to Brimpts."

"Oh, I have nothing else to do, and I like a drive."

"With me? — or perhaps I just spoil the pleasure,"
Rose asked, with a roguish look out of the corners of her
eyes.

The young yeoman was unaccustomed to making gallant
speeches, and he let slip the opportunity thus adroitly offered
him. Rose curled her lip, as he replied—

"It is always pleasanter to have someone to talk to than
to be alone, especially for a long drive."

"But it is so good, so *very* good of you to fetch *her*."

"Why should I be such a churl as not to go when
asked?"

"After what has occurred, you know. What a fellow you
are! In the orchard, you know."

Pooke turned blood-red. A fly was tickling him; he
raised the butt-end of his whip and rubbed his nose with it.

"Get along, Tucker!" he shouted. Tucker was the horse.

"I hope I shall profit better from your example than I have from all the parson's sermons," pursued Rose.

"What are you at?" asked Pooke uneasily, conscious that some ulterior end was in his companion's view, as she thus lavished encomiums on him, and then dug into his nerves a needlepoint of sharp remark.

"What am I at? Oh, Jan! nothing at all, but sitting here with my hands in my lap, so happy to have a drive—and in such excellent company—company so good."

"I don't understand what you mean."

"It is not every man would lend his cart, nay, drive himself, to do a favour to a girl who had treated him outrageously."

"When did you treat me so?"

"I—oh, Jan—not I! I could not have done that. A thousand times no"— Rose spoke in pretty agitation, and fluttered at his side. "I mean Kitty."

"Kitty? Get along, Tucker!—it's no use your trying to scratch yourself with your hind hoof, and run at the same time." He addressed the horse, which was executing awkward gymnastics. "Excuse me, Rose; I must dismount. There is a briar stinging Tucker."

Jan drew up, descended, and slapped with his open hand where a horse-fly was engaged sucking blood. The fly was too wide awake to be killed; it rose, and sailed away. Then young Pooke mounted again.

"Get along, Tucker!" he said, and applied the whip.

"I mean," pursued Rose, as if there had ensued no interruption. "I mean, after you had been treated so shamefully."

"I didn't know it."

"Really, Jan! Everyone knows that Kitty refused you. It is the village talk, and everyone says it was scandalous."

"Drat it! there is that fly again at Tucker."

"Oh, if you can think of nothing but Tucker, I'll be silent."

"Don't be cross, Rose, I must consider Tucker, as I am driver. There might be accidents."

"Not for the world. Of course you must consider Tucker, and poor little I must be content to come into your mind in the loops and gaps not took up by the horse and the gadfly."

"What do you suppose Tucker cost father?" asked Pooke, clumsily endeavouring to change the topic.

"I really don't know."

"Eight pounds, and he is worth twenty. That was a piece of luck for father."

"Luck comes to those who desarve it," said Rose. "I am not surprised at you and your family being prosperous in all you undertake. There's no knowing, Jan,"—she spoke solemnly,—"you may feel low and discouraged at being, so to speak, kicked over the orchard hedge by Kate, but it may be a blessing in disguise, who can tell? but Providence may have in view someone for you much better suited—*much* in every way, than Kitty."

"Drat it! there is that fly again."

"Mr. Puddicombe—what a good soul he is!—has been about the place spreading the news."

"What news?"

"About Kitty and the schoolmaster."

"Kitty and the schoolmaster?" echoed Pooke. His brows went up, his jaw dropped, and his cheek became mottled.

"Haven't you heard? Why, poor dear Jan, she went helter-skelter away from the orchard where she had trampled on you to fling herself into the arms of Mr. Thingamy-jig. I cannot tell his name—I mean the new schoolmaster."

"How do you know?"

"Of course I know. Mr. Puddicombe is brimming with the news. They went like a pair of turtle-doves cooing and billing to Mr. Puddicombe, and he has nearly run his legs down to stumps since. The schoolmaster"—

"But I don't mean about the schoolmaster." Pooke spoke with a tremble in his voice.

"Oh! about that affair, that comical affair in the orchard? Half the village, I reckon, was out behind the hedges looking and listening. There was Betsy Baker, and there was Jenny Jones, and that sprig of a chap, Tommy Croft—I won't be sure they heard, but I fancy so—anyhow, everyone has been talking of it, and pitying you that you were made ridiculous; and then to go off, right on end, and accept a schoolmaster." In a tone of infinite contempt, Rose added, "A schoolmaster! It takes ten tailors to make a man, and ten schoolmasters

to make a tailor; Puddicombe excepted—that was a man,
and was so highly respected, he knew how to make himself
looked up to, and folk forgave him his profession for his
own sake. But this new whipper-snapper! And to be
rejected for *him*!"

Jan Pooke writhed. He had not heard the news of
Kate's engagement. Somehow it had been kept from, or
had not reached, him. The fire had distracted men's and
women's thoughts from the affairs of Kate, Bramber, and
himself. His colour changed, and he flushed purple. He
shared the prejudice entertained by farmers and labourers
—by all who were semi-educated and wholly uneducated
—for the man of culture that was striving to enlighten dull
minds and wake torpid intelligences. Parsons and schoolmasters are in the same category. The heavy soul resents being raised to spiritual life, and the heavy mind
resents being wakened to intellectual life. It ever will
be so, and it ever has been so. A man going along a road
found a sodden toper lying in a ditch. He tried to pull
him out. "Leave alone!" roared the drunken man. "I
likes it, I enjoys it. I'll knock you down if you don't let
me lie in my ditch. There are effets there, and slugs
there, and frogs and toads; get along your own way and
leave me where I am."

Pooke and Rose Ash had imbibed the views of their
parents and companions, and the prevailing atmosphere in
a country parish. They had not risen above it, and their
ideas took colour from it.

"It was scandalous conduct, was it not, Jan?" asked

Rose. "If I were you, I wouldn't stand it, not half an hour."

"But what can I do?"

"What—? do—? Oh, lots!"

"I can do lots. I do not see it. If Kitty chooses"— His lips quivered, and he gulped down something.

"If Kitty chooses a beggarly schoolmaster instead of you, you must not let the neighbours see you are crest-fallen. It will never do in coming out of church for everyone to point at you and say, 'Poor chap! There he goes, Jan Pooke, whom Kitty Alone would not have; and here comes Mr. Thingamy-jig, whom she prefers so highly, looking like the cock of the walk.' It would be very shaming, Jan, and I don't think your dear father would like it terrible much."

"I can do nothing," said Jan, looking wistfully at the horse's ears : "if Kitty likes Mr. Bramber, and don't care for me."

"And if the story of the silver peninks gets about?"

"Don't, Rose!" His face expressed pain.

"I don't wish to hurt you, I wish you well, Jan, you know. I was anxious that you should not be the laughing-stock of Coombe and the neighbourhood. That would be too dreadful. I have such a regard for you. Mind you, I love dear Kitty, but I cannot blind my eyes that her has made a mistake—a happy mistake for you, because, dear, good girl as she is, I do not think that she could ha' made you happy."

"Why not?"

"She would have been eternally axin' questions which you could never answer."

"There is something in that."

"She'd have been wanting to take you to the bottoms of wells, you know, so as to see the stars by day. You would not like that, Jan?"

"No—there is something in that."

"And to make you read that stupid book—Wordsworth, her calls it — in the evening, whilst she knitted. You couldn't have stood that, Jan?"

"Horrible !—I should ha' died."

"Then you may rejoice that Providence has ordained that she should go after the schoolmaster. Now you must look out and see what step you can take to recover the respect of the parish."

"How can I do that?"

"Oh, there be more fishes in the sea than come out of it, I reckon."

Jan remained in meditation, speechless. Rose pressed close to his side.

"Have you no room?" he asked.

"Oh, 'tisn't that altogether; my feelings overcame me. I do so, so pity you, you dear, poor Jan."

Presently, as he continued silent, she said, "If I were you, when shortly you meet Kitty, and when she will be in my place at your side, and I ride behind, I would not look like an apple that has gone under the rollers, nor hang my ears like a whipped dog, but laugh and joke and whistle and be jolly, you know."

"That don't seem right, with her father burned to death."

"She knows nothing of that, and is to know nothing of it from us. The proper person to tell her is Mrs. Pepperill. So mind, Jan, not a word about Mr. Quarm. Understand, not a word. So look cheerful and whistle."

"What shall I whistle? Jackson's 'Tee-dum'?"

"Of course not, something lively. The 'Green Bushes.'"

"Why the 'Green Bushes'?"

"Oh, silly Jan!" Then she began to sing—

> "'The old lover arrived, the maiden was gone;
> He sighed very deeply, he stood all alone,
> "She is on with another, before off with me,
> So adieu ye green bushes for ever!" said he.'

"Green bushes—that is the orchard, Jan, where grow the silver peninks."

"Drat that fly!" exclaimed Jan, flicking with his whip. "Her's at it again."

CHAPTER XL

A GREAT FEAR

KATE was among the felled timber at Brimpts, skip-
ping about the logs, stooping, then rising again,
and withal singing merrily, when Jan and Rose, having
put up the horse at Dart-meet, came up the valley to join
her.

The peeled trunks lay white as bones on the surface of
the moor, and a fresh and stimulating odour was exhaled
from them. The bark was piled up in stacks at intervals.
The whortleberry was flowering in the spring sun. The
heather was still dead. Horns of ferns, brown, and curled
like pastoral staves, stood up between the trunks.

After the first greetings had been exchanged, Rose
asked Kitty, "What in the world are you doing here—
bobbing about? In search of long cripples (vipers)?"

"No; I do not want them. I have started some
basking in the hot sun, but they slip away at once and do
no harm. I am counting the rings on the trees."

"What for?"

"To learn their age."

"Who cares how old the trees are?"

"I do; and thus one can find out in what years the trees grew fast, and which summers were wet and cold."

"Really, Kitty, you are going silly."

"It is interesting," pursued Kate; "and then, Rose, I do not altogether believe in the rings telling the age truly. I think the oaks are much older than they pretend to be."

"Like old maids?" suggested Rose.

"Yes, Rose; after a certain age they cease to grow— cease to swell, they just live on as they were, or go back in their hearts, then they make no rings. The rings tell you for how many years they went on expanding, but say nothing about those when they were at a standstill. Then, look here : the rings are on one side much thicker than on the other, and that is because of a cold and stormy wind. They thicken their bark against the wind, just as I might put on a shawl."

"Oh,—by the way—touching a shawl "—

But Kate was too eager and interested in her subject to bear interruption.

"I have the oddest and most wonderful thing to show you, Rose. You do not care about the rings, but this you will be truly pleased to see."

"What is that?"

"Follow me."

Kate skipped among the prostrate oaks till she reached one large trunk. As she skipped, she sang merrily—-

"'All in the wood there grew a fine tree.'"

"What song is that, Kate?" asked Rose.

"It is one that the head woodcutter taught me.

> ' All in the wood there grew a fine tree,
>   The finest tree that ever you might see,
>   And the green leaves flourished around.'

All on this tree there grew a fine bough, and all on this bough there grew a fine twig. Then it goes on to tell how on this twig there was a fine nest, and how in this nest there was a fine bird, the finest bird that ever you did see; and on this bird there grew a fine feather, and out of the feather was made a fine bed, and on this fine bed was laid a fine babe, and out of the babe there grew a fine man, and the man put an acorn into the earth, and out of the acorn there grew a fine tree, and the tree was of the acorn, and the acorn of the man, and the man was from the babe, and the babe was on the bed, and the bed was of the feather, and the feather of the bird, and the bird was in the nest, and the nest was on the twig, and the twig was on the bough, and the bough was on the tree, and the tree was in the wood.

> ' And the green leaves flourished around—around—around,
>   And the green leaves flourished around.'"

"What nonsense, Kate!"

"It is not nonsense. There is a great deal in it. The song goes on without an end, always the same; just as at the end of the psalm, 'As it was in the beginning, is now, and ever shall be.' See!—this is what I have to show you."

She pointed to some lettering that ran round the white

peeled trunk, brown as coffee ; somewhat large and strained the characters seemed, and Rose was not able to decipher them, but she said—

"However came letters to be there, under the bark ? "

"That is the great curiosity," answered Kate. "Some-one cut them in the bark with his knife when the tree was young, two hundred years ago. The tree has grown big since then, and has healed up its wounds, but still bears the scars; and it has drawn its bark round it, and for years upon years has hidden what was written from the eyes of man. Only now that the dear old oak is hewn down, and the bark stripped away, is the writing revealed which was cut on it two hundred years ago."

"What are the words ? "

" Listen—I have spelled them out.

> 'O Tree defying Time
> Witness bear
> That two loving Hearts
> 1643
> Did meet here.'

Is not this wonderful ? The tree was trusted, and it has fulfilled its trust, and would have done so till it died. Two hundred years ago, two young lovers met here, and the youth cut this on the bark. Two hundred years after, it gives up its witness. If it had not been cut down, two hundred years hence it would have done the same."

Rose looked at Jan, and took his hand and sighed.

"Jan, let us sit down on this tree. This touches me; does it not you, Jan?"

"What—your hand?"

"No, silly; I mean this about the lovers."

Then Kate began to sing—

> " ' All in the wood there grew a fine tree,
> The finest tree that ever you did see,
> And the green leaves flourished around.' "

Then Kate said, clapping her hands—

"Is there not a great deal in that song of the tree in the wood? I suppose in paradise that Adam stood by the tree of life and felt happy when he held Eve by the hand and looked into her eyes. If he could have written, he would have cut these same words in the bark of the tree of life. And years went by, and it was always and ever the same story: the young grew old, and then others came in their places, and loving hearts met, and again and again in an endless whirl, and an ever-returning tide, and a perpetual circling of the stars in heaven, and the new flowers coming after the old have died—'As it was in the beginning, is now, and ever shall be.'"

Then Jan started up, drew his hand from Rose, and said—

"We have come for you, Kitty. As soon as the horse has had a feed, we must be off."

"Is there such a terrible hurry?" asked Rose with a tone of reproach in her voice.

"We have no time to lose."

"Lose, Jan?"

"To waste, I mean."

"Waste, Jan?"

"I mean—bother it!—we must be off as soon as the horse is a bit rested. We have a long journey to take, up and down, and little trotting ground. We have come for Kitty. You must return with us," looking at Kate. "There has been something"—

"Let me speak," interrupted Rose, afraid lest Pooke should let out too much. "Kitty, your uncle and aunt have met with a great loss. The stores have been burnt, and Mrs. Zerah does nothing but sob and cry after you."

"Auntie cry for me?"

"Yes. She will not be at rest till you return."

"I'll go at once," said Kate, flushing with pleasure. "When did this happen?"

"Tuesday night."

"That is the night we came here. Is my father at the Cellars?"

"I have not seen him. Now, Jan"— Pooke was about to speak. Rose stopped his mouth. "Leave me to speak. You are a blunderer."

"But I know he passed us going to Coombe," said Kate.

"Passed you—where?"

"On the hill. We were in the linhay."

Rose held out a shawl.

"Kitty, is this yours?"

"Yes; it is. I lost it on my way here. Where did you find it?"

" In the linhay in Furze Park. I went there with our cow, Buttercup. The calf is taken from her. There I found it."

" We turned into the field, and I remained a long time in the linhay," said Kate.

" And your uncle?"

" Oh, he went back to the Cellars."

" What, by the road?"

" No; by the waterside. I was tired, and the time was long, or I thought it was; so I folded my shawl to keep the prickles from my head,—there is so much furze there,— and I lay down and slept."

" I found this also," said Rose, extending a match-box. " I don't understand what it is."

" It is a lucifer-box. My uncle had it. He pulled a match across something, and it blazed up. I suppose he dropped it in the linhay, also, whilst getting the horse and cart out."

" What! you had horse and cart there?"

" Yes."

" And your uncle went back to the Cellars?"

" Yes; just before. Indeed, as we turned into the field, I heard my father go by; I heard him speak to Neddy. He always talks to the donkey as he goes along."

" You did not speak to your father?"

" No. Uncle was impatient, and father was rattling along at a fine pace, and you know from that place it is all down hill to Coombe."

" Your uncle returned to the Cellars after that; you are quite sure of it?"

"Yes; certain. He told me he had forgotten to lock up."

"Why did he not go by the road?"

"I cannot tell—perhaps he thought the other way shortest."

"It is not that. Was he long away?"

"I cannot tell. I fell asleep. Have you not anything to tell me of father? I know he went to Coombe."

"I have told you—I have not seen him."

"Where can he be?"

Neither answered that question.

Even into Jan's dull brain there penetrated an idea that some mystery connected with Pasco Pepperill was involved —that it was singular that he, his wife, and niece should have all left the Cellars before the fire broke out, and that Pasco should have returned there secretly after having left. He said nothing. If he tried to think, his thoughts became entangled, and he saw nothing clearly. An uneasy feeling pervaded him, which he was unable to explain to himself.

During the first part of the journey back to the Cellars, Kate talked. She sat beside Jan Pooke. Rose was behind, keeping a ready ear to hear what was said, and interfere should she deem it expedient.

"Where can my father be?" asked Kitty.

As no answer was given to her query, she said further—

"It is very strange, and I cannot understand how he is not there. He must have been at Coombe just before the fire broke out. I know he passed along the road. Where are the donkey and cart?"

"They are at the Cellars," answered Jan.

"Then my father must be there. He cannot be far off. He cannot get about easily, as he is so lame."

"I suppose he must be somewhere," was the wise observation of Pooke.

"Hasn't my aunt seen him?"

"No, Kitty."

"Nor anyone."

Jan hesitated, and presently said—

"I did hear something about the parson having spoke with her, but I don't know the rights of it."

"He must be there. He cannot be far off. We shall see him when we arrive. I daresay he had some business that took him off; but if he heard of the fire, he would come back at once. He will be a loser by it as well as my uncle."

"Folk say there will be no loss, as Mr. Pepperill insured so terrible heavy. They do tell that he has insured for two thousand pounds, and that only about fifty pounds worth of goods is burnt."

Kate shrank together. Rose touched Pooke significantly to hold his tongue.

After that Kitty remained very silent. A feeling of unrest took possession of her, even of alarm, at some impending catastrophe. That her uncle had been in difficulty she knew. That he was in want of money to pay for the timber before he could realise on it, and to meet his dishonoured bill for the wool, she knew. A chill ran through her veins.

After a long period of silence Rose said to her—

"Kitty, is it true that you and the schoolmaster went to old Mr. Puddicombe about being engaged?"

"Yes," answered the girl addressed.

"He took it as a mark of proper respect?"

"Yes."

"Jan, dear," said Rose, touching Pooke, "as soon as we get to Coombe, you and I will go and call on Mr. Puddicombe. It will please him. He was the first who heard about your engagement, Kitty?"

"Not quite that—we told Mr. Fielding."

"Oh, the parson! But everyone respects Mr. Puddicombe *so* much, that I think Jan and I will go to him first. You know, Kitty, we have settled it between us— I mean, Jan and I—on our way to Brimpts, and Mr. Puddicombe ought to know."

CHAPTER XLI

I T was evening when Kate was driven up to the Cellars, yet not so dark but that she could see the donkey in the paddock, and dark enough to make the glow of the still smoking heap visible, here and there, in red seams and yellow sparks.

"There is Neddy," exclaimed Kate. "My father must be here."

As she was descending from the cart, she said, "Why, he may have crossed the Teign in the boat."

"No, Kitty," answered Jan; "I don't think that."

"Why not?"

Pooke was afraid ot answering lest he should involve himself; and Rose had jumped down at the mill, and so was not there to prevent him from committing an error.

Before entering the house, in her anxiety about her father, Kate ran to the mooring-place of the boats, and came back in some exultation to Jan. "I said so. He has crossed. The old boat is gone."

"It was there yesterday. It was there all the night of

45

the fire and next day. It has been taken since," answered Pooke.

Kate was downcast. She held out her hand to Jan, took her little bundle, and entered the house. Her aunt had not come out to meet her. That she had not expected. No one in that house had shown her graciousness and desire for her presence, and she had ceased to expect it.

When she entered, it was with a hesitating foot. She thought that Rose, out of good nature and desire to please, had represented her aunt as more desirous to have her than she really was. Having never met with affection on the part of Zerah, hardly with recognition of her services, she did not anticipate a complete change in demeanour. She was surprised to find that her aunt had not lighted a candle.

She called to her, when Zerah replied, with a cry that thrilled Kate to her heart's core, "Is that my Kitty? My child come back to me?"

In another moment aunt and niece were locked in each other's arms, and sobbing out their hearts,—Kate, through joy, dashed with dread of evil; Zerah, through joy at seeing her niece again, a joy that sprang out of despair.

A singular relation now developed itself between them. After a very short while, Kitty perceived that there was something on her aunt's mind, that Zerah was weighed down with a sense of some calamity far exceeding that of the loss of so many tons of coal and so many fleeces of wool. The woman was suddenly become timid and apprehensive. It gave her pain to speak of what had taken

place, and she avoided by every kind of subterfuge express-
ing an opinion as to the cause of the fire, and as to the
extent of the damage done.   She had for some years faced
the prospect of financial ruin, and if this had come upon
her, Kate was sure she would have met it, not indeed with
equanimity, but with sullen assurance that it was inevitable,
and have prepared herself to accept the new position of
poverty.

But that which occupied and disorganised the heart of
Zerah was something else, something more fearful.   Kate
saw that she shrank not only from allusion to the fire, but
from inquiries as to the fate of her brother, and whenever
Jason was named or referred to, the woman caught her
niece to her bosom and covered her with kisses, wept,
trembled, but said nothing.

Mrs. Pepperill took Kate from her little attic-room to
share her bed during the absence of Pasco, and the girl
found that the trouble which weighed on her aunt during
the day haunted and tortured her during the night.   Zerah
slept little, tossed in her bed; and if she slept, broke into
moans and exclamations.

Meanwhile, Kitty did not rest from making inquiries
relative to her father.   She visited the rector, and ascertained from his lips that he had seen and exchanged words
with Jason Quarm on the evening of the fire, in fact, only
an hour or two before the fire must have broken out.

But where was her father?   The old boat was gone, that
was true; but it was in its place on the morning after the
fire, as well as all that night.   It had been taken later;

and there was, perhaps, not much to marvel at in this, when the Cellars were crowded with all conditions of sight-seers and mischief-doers pervading the precincts. Dishonest men might have taken advantage of the confusion to purloin the boat, or mischievous boys to have loosed the cable and let her drift with the tide where it chose to sweep her.

Inevitably Kate became aware of the opinion prevailing in the village, that her father was burned to death in the storehouse, and it was hard for her to come to any other conclusion. She went to Mrs. Redmore to inquire whether he had been to his old cottage, but the timid, not very bright woman nervously denied any knowledge of him.

Her distress was very great, but she sought to conceal it from her aunt, who wanted nothing to augment her own trouble.

Hitherto the fire had smouldered on in the ruins, but it became less, and though the charred masses still gave out gusts of heat, there was no more smoke rising from them, only a quivering of the air above the ashes.

The fire was naturally the main topic of conversation in the neighbourhood. Minds as well as tongues were exercised. Comments were made on the absence of Pasco, which were rendered hardly more favourable by the knowledge that he had gone to a funeral. He knew nothing of his uncle's illness and death when he started. Why had he sent his wife away? Why had he carried his niece back to Dartmoor, from which she had been recently brought?

Incautious exclamations of Zerah, when first made aware

of the fire and of her brother's disappearance, together with her reticence since, were discussed.

Prowlers came round the house, peering into this part, then another. An agent from the insurance office suddenly presented himself, listened to and noted down the various rumours in circulation, and threw out a hint that his office would consider before it paid the sum for which the store-house and its contents were inscribed.

The rector called on Mrs. Pepperill, and without appearing to intrude on her troubles, endeavoured to gain from her something which might elucidate the mystery of Quarm's disappearance. Her mouth remained shut, and her eyes scrutinised him with suspicion.

Mr. Pooke senior was constable, and he considered it his duty to intervene. He owed a grudge, nay, two, to Pasco Pepperill, and this fire was an opportunity for paying it off. He was angry with Pepperill because he had not shown him the deference that Pooke considered his due, and had wrested from him the office of churchwarden. A triumph indeed would it prove were he to be able to make Pepperill amenable to the law. Moreover, Pepperill was uncle to the chit who had dared—positively dared!—to refuse his son. He had not desired the engagement—he had disliked the idea of it—he would have vastly preferred his son's union with the miller's daughter. But that Pepperill's niece—the daughter of that donkey-driver, Jason Quarm—should have the temerity to refuse his son was a fact he could not stomach; it was a spot in his mantle of pride.

When he heard the talk about Pepperill, he considered himself justified—nay, called upon by virtue of his office—to make himself acquainted with all the facts, and, if possible, to get his rival into difficulties. A rival Pepperill was. Pooke regarded himself as a sort of king in Coombe, where his family had held lands for centuries; never, indeed, extending the patrimony; never suing for a grant of arms, but holding on to the paternal acres as yeomen—substantial, self-esteeming, defiant of new-comers.

Pasco was not exactly in this latter category, but he was a man who gave himself great airs, who showed the yeoman no deference, and took a delight in thwarting him, and heading a clique against him at vestry, and generally in the parish.

Pooke listened attentively to all that was said relative to the fire, and prejudice against the man induced him to believe that Pasco had fired his own stores in order to obtain the insurance money; by what means Quarm was made the victim he could not tell. If he could prove Pepperill to be a rascal, it would be great satisfaction, but if he proved him to be a villain guilty of murder, that would be ecstasy.

Without warning given to Mrs. Pepperill, Mr. Pooke made a descent on the Cellars, attended by four of his men armed with shovels and picks. He did not even ask her leave to overturn the ruins and search among the heaps of ash for the remains of the man who, it was surmised, had perished in the fire. With an imperious voice and a consequential air he gave his orders; and when the men were engaged in testing the cinders to find whether they were cool, and might safely be turned over, and in hacking and removing the beams charred and menacing a fall, he betook himself to the outhouse, where was the cart, so as to examine that.

He returned speedily, carrying a bundle fastened in a handkerchief, and this he proceeded to open. It contained a clean shirt, stockings, a razor, and other articles such as a man would be likely to take with him when about to stay abroad a night or two.

"There!" exclaimed Pooke. "I have found at once what no one else saw—indubitable evidence not only that Jason Quarm came here, but that he never left this place. If he is not under these cinders, I ask, where else can he be?"

Kate and her aunt looked out at the door timidly. They knew that Mr. Pooke was constable, and they had no idea of any limit to his authority. He came towards them.

"I must know all about it—the ins and outs; the ups and downs. No blinking with me—no rolling of the matter up in blather. What do you know of Jason Quarm?" He turned to Mrs. Pepperill.

"Nothing at all," she answered. "I do not even know that he came here."

"Come here he did," said Pooke. "Here is the donkey —here the cart—here his bundle of clothes. Now, did he go away?"

"I was not here; I was at Teignmouth. I know nothing," said Zerah in nervous terror.

"The girl—the girl who had the impudence—to—to

refuse my son—she knows something about this! She was with her uncle. Why did he ask Mr. Ash, the miller, to not only date his receipt of a trifle by the day of month, but by the hour of the evening? That is not ordinarily done. And why did he sneak back to the Cellars, after he had got a little way along the road, putting his trap up, and leaving it with the girl? I want to know all that!"

"Here is my uncle; he will answer you himself," gasped Kitty, perplexed and alarmed at the string of questions, and then relieved to see Pasco arrive.

"What is the meaning of this?" shouted Pepperill, jumping out of a hired conveyance. He was in profound mourning, very new and glossy. "What is this you are doing, Pooke? Where is your authority?"

"I am constable."

"A constable without a warrant! Off!—leave my ground at once! I'll communicate with my solicitor, and have a summons taken out against you. My solicitor is not a man to understand jokes—nor am I."

"You may be in the right for the moment," said Pooke, becoming purple with vexation at being caught going beyond his powers, and with anger at being sent off, when he had come to the spot with such blare and blaze of authority. "But I'll tell you what it is, Master Pepperill, there are queer tales abroad about you and this fire, and we want to know, where is Jason Quarm?"

"Quarm?—gone to Portsmouth."

"To Portsmouth?"

"Of course; we are in treaty with the dockyard for our timber at Brimpts."

"I don't believe it! He is burnt!—here!"

"Burnt? Fudge! He said he was going to Portsmouth."

"He said that? When did you see him?"

"I mean I heard from him to that effect. Now be off! I'll have no overhauling of my premises! I'll have no cross-questioning here! I have a solicitor of my own now, and he shall know the reason of everything. Get you gone! —and be blowed!"

CHAPTER XLII

TALKING loudly, laughing noisily, boisterously threatening proceedings against all trespassers, Pasco Pepperill came in at his door.

"For heaven's sake, what are you doing?" was his first salutation from his wife. "How dare you behave as you do? You—you?"

He saw at once that she believed in his guilt, and designed to caution him against overacting his part.

A great transformation had taken place in Pepperill. Now that he had done the deed, all dread of the consequences seemed to have been swept away; he must assume an innocent part, look people full in the face, and resent suspicion as an insult. The fact that he had come in for a handsome legacy assisted him to shake off the consciousness of guilt. He was now a man worth three or four thousand pounds, and when the assurance was paid he would be worth an additional thousand.

What could be proved against him? Nothing. Suspicion might be entertained, but what was suspicion when it had nothing substantial as a basis?

"Give me a jug of cider," he commanded, and Zerah hastened to obey. She put a tumbler on the table beside the jug.

Pasco leisurely poured out a glass, and held it up between himself and the light, and was pleased to observe how steady his hand was.

"Zerah! come and look here. There is rope in the liquor—it is turning sour."

Kate looked fixedly at her uncle's face. The child was in distress and doubt. Was her father alive, or had he died a death of the worst description? Was he away on his business, carrying out some risky speculation, or did his bones lie resolved to ash in the great cinder-heap that had smouldered on so long, and was but just extinct?

She had not met with anything in her uncle's character which would justify her in attributing to him so deliberate and desperate a crime as firing his own warehouse, and sacrificing, intentionally or accidentally, the life of his brother-in-law; and yet his wife, who ought to know him best, had arrived at the worst conclusion, and though she said nothing, Kate saw by her manner that she was for ever estranged from her husband, and regarded him as guilty of the crime in its worst form.

Zerah had retained Kitty in her room, and had more than once said to her that after the return of Pasco she would make him occupy Kate's old attic; she would no longer treat Pasco other than as a stranger. Her reception of him now showed repugnance and restraint; the shrinking of an upright nature from one tainted with dishonesty, and exhibiting restraint from saying all that was felt.

Kate looked on her uncle with his self-satisfied expression, holding the glass between him and the light with a steady hand, concerning his mind about the ropiness of the cider, and in her simple mind, ignorant of evil, direct, with no trickiness or dissimulation in it, she felt vast relief. She could not believe that Pasco had done wrong, nor that he had any misgivings as to the well-being of her father.

She drew a long sigh, and passed her hand across her brow, as though to brush away the cloud that had hung over it and darkened all her thoughts.

In the new confidence established between herself and her aunt, Kate had whispered to her that she was engaged to Walter Bramber, but the news seemed to make as little impression on Zerah as it had on Pasco, and for the same reason, that each mind was engrossed in other more immediately interesting matters. The girl submitted with that resignation which characterised her. She made little account of herself, and did not suppose that what concerned her could excite lively emotions in the hearts of her uncle and aunt. Even Mr. Puddicombe had shown more sympathy and pleasure. But then, Kate could make allowance for the preoccupation of her aunt's mind consequent on the fire.

Kate now timidly approached her uncle, keeping her eyes riveted on his face, and, standing on the other side of the little round table on which was his jug, she asked—

"Are you quite sure my dear father is all right?"

Pasco looked sharply at her.

"Questions again?" he said hastily, and a flush came into his cheek.

"I have a right to ask this question," said Kate firmly.

His eye fell under hers; he set down the glass unsteadily and upset the cider.

"Hang it! why have you a right?"

"I want to know that my father is alive."

"I say he's gone to Portsmouth."

"But how did he go?"

"That was his affair, not mine; the Atmospheric, I suppose."

"He could not cross during that night—at least, not till near dawn, and so must have been here when the warehouse was burnt."

"I don't see that; there are other ways of getting away. He went on to Shaldon."

That was certainly possible. Quarm might have pursued the right bank of the river to where it could be crossed at any tide, but this was not probable.

An interruption was occasioned by the entry of the rector. After the usual salutations, he at once turned to the topic which had been engaging thoughts and tongues before he appeared.

"I have no desire to intrude," said he, "but I have come to prevent a scandal, if possible, and perhaps a quarrel. Mr. Pooke is in a great heat, and vows he will have a search-warrant to turn over the heaps, as you have refused him to explore them. You are churchwarden, Mr. Pepperill, and

I not only desire to prevent unpleasantness on your own account, but on that of the Church. You have, I believe, sent Mr. Pooke off?"

"I have."

"But why so? He may have acted irregularly, but it was with good intentions, and you were absent."

"He had no right to touch what was mine."

"No doubt he erred, but you were absent, consider; and your wife, your niece, the whole village, were in excitement and alarm. He did what seemed fit to allay this unrest; to find out whether Mr. Quarm had been here or not."

"It is no good. He'll get no warrant, unless magistrates be fools. He has no case—not a ghost of a case. Jason went to Shaldon, and so over the water."

"You are sure?"

"I fancy he did. I heard he wanted to reach Portsmouth, and the tide was out when he got here, so he could not cross in the ferry. He went on. At Teignmouth he would get into the Atmospheric."

"That is readily ascertained. We have but to send to Shaldon and inquire. The boatman who took him across can be found. If he crossed the wooden bridge, then the man who takes toll will be able to say something."

"He may have gone round the head of the estuary."

"Not likely, if he left his cart and donkey here."

Pepperill was unable to answer. He was a heavy-headed man, not quick at invention.

"Then," continued the rector, "the warehouse did not catch fire of itself; someone must have fired it."

"Of course," said Pepperill.

"I may as well tell you," continued Mr. Fielding, "that Mr. Bramber, the schoolmaster, came to the Cellars the evening of the fire"—

"The deuce he did!"

"Just after dusk."

"And what brought him here, the puppy?"

"He came," answered Mr. Fielding, "because he wished to see Kitty and you."

"Pray what did he want with Kitty?"

"Surely, Mr. Pepperill, you know that the two young people have come to an understanding."

Pasco shrugged his shoulders. "I may have heard something of the sort, but I have other things more important to interest and occupy my mind. I gave it no heed."

"Well, he desired to speak with you, as her father was away, and you stood in a semi-parental relation to her, living as she did in your house."

"Well, he found no one here," observed Pasco, with some uneasiness of manner.

"As he approached the Cellars he heard an altercation, and then the house door violently slammed. Then, thinking the occasion unpropitious, he turned back."

"It was fancy. No one was here. My wife was over the water, and I on my way to Brimpts. If you doubt my word, ask Mr. Ash, he receipted my bill, and I had a talk as well with the landlord."

"That is true, Mr. Pepperill, but Jason Quarm was here. I saw him drive past my gate, and I cast a good-even to him. If an altercation took place here, he was probably one of those engaged in it. I took it for granted that you were the other."

"I—I—I?" stuttered Pasco.

"Yes, because you returned to the Cellars after you had got to the head of the hill."

"Who said that? It is a lie!"

"Kitty, I understand, said as much to John Pooke."

"Kitty said it?"

"Kitty told Jan and Rose as she was being driven home from the moor—so I have been .nformed."

"It's a lie!" roared Pasco, glaring round at the girl with a curl up of his thick lips, showing his teeth like a dog about to bite. "It's a —— lie!"

"Mr. Pepperill!" said the rector, rising in dignified anger from the seat that had been accorded him, "I will not suffer you to use such an expression in my presence, even in your own house. You do not add one jot to the force of your repudiation—to your charge against Kate—by burdening it with an oath."

"It's like that beggarly schoolmaster's impudence to come poking his snout here, where he's not wanted, where "—with some energy—"I won't have him! I'll have the law of him for trespass!"

"He did not trespass. It is free to anyone to approach a house door."

"I don't care; I'll shoot him if he shows his face here again."

"You are branching away from the matter in immediate

consideration. There seems to be a conflict of testimony. Kitty, whom I have always found true and direct as a needle, has made one statement,—not indeed to me, but to others,—and this you contradict."

"I'm churchwarden—I'm a man of means and in a good business. I should think my word was worth more than that of a sly, chattering, idle minx."

"Sly, chattering, that my little Kitty is not; I have ever found her straightforward and reserved. As to her work in the house, her aunt is better qualified to express an opinion than you, Mr. Pepperill."

"I don't see that you've any call to come here, poking into matters and axin' questions like another Kitty, if I may make so bold as to say so," said Pasco, defiant and then qualifying his defiance.

"As I told you at the outset, Mr. Pepperill, I have come here not to make an official inquiry, but to prevent one. There is a mistake somewhere. My wish was to clear it up before matters grew to a head. You and Mr. Pooke are both stubborn men, and may knock heads and crack skulls over nothing. A word will probably lighten what is now dark, and dissipate a growing mistrust. I cannot, and I will not, believe half of what is being said relative to you. I have come to your house as a peacemaker, to entreat you to so account for little matters which puzzle the good people here, before what is now whispered may be brayed, what is now a conjecture may be crystallised into a conviction. As far as is known, the matter stands thus: Mr. Quarm came here, and here have been found his donkey and cart and his little bundle of clothes. If he had crossed the water, he would have taken the latter with him. Two persons were heard in altercation here shortly after his having passed through Coombe, and the door was shut violently. Next morning the door was locked, and Mrs. Pepperill when she came found the key in a hiding-place known, as she then said, only to herself and you."

"Don't you suppose Kitty knew it also?"

"I daresay she did. Your wife's words, when she arrived, found the stores burnt, and the house locked, and the key in a certain place—her words were, 'Pasco has put the key where I have found it.' It was of course surmised that before you left you had locked the door, but Kitty told young Pooke that when you reached the top of the hill you returned to the Cellars, saying that you had forgotten to lock the house. It, therefore, seemed to me probable that on your return, you and Quarm came to high words about something."

"Nothing of the sort I never came back."

"Oh, uncle!" escaped Kate's lips.

He turned his menacing eyes on her, with the same snarl on his mouth.

"I'll tell you the truth, the whole truth, and nothing but the truth," said he. "That is, if you will insist on having it, and you can make of it what you like, pass'n. When I got to the top o' the hill, where is Ash's linhay, it is true that I remembered I'd not locked up the dwelling-house. Then I sent Kitty back and told her to lock and put the key where her aunt would find it, and I'd stay and mind the hoss."

"Uncle!" Kitty turned white and rigid.

"And, dash it! if someone must ha' set fire to the old place,—and I reckon there was someone, them things don't do themselves,—it must ha' been either she or Jason, or both together. And I reckon he's run away to escape the consequences."

The rector stood up. He had reseated himself after his protest. His face was very grave.

"I see," said he, taking his hat, and moving to the door. "This affair wears a different colour from what I supposed. It must be elucidated irrespective of me. My part is done. It must be taken up and investigated by the proper authorities."

CHAPTER XLIII

MUCH CRY AND A LITTLE WOOL

"AUNT!" exclaimed Kitty, blank and trembling, turning to Zerah, the moment the rector had left the house. "Oh, auntie dear, this is not true—this that Uncle Pasco says. I did not go back. I was left in the linhay with the cart. What does he mean?"

"He means to shelter himself," answered Mrs. Pepperill. Then the woman stepped in front of her husband, and, in her harshest tones and hardest manner, said, "Pasco! A yea or nay from Kitty is, as pass'n said, worth a thousand of your protestations, though bolstered up wi' oaths."

"Of course Kitty is everything to you and the pass'n, and I am nothing. I know that very well. I've had enough of your violence o' tongue-lash these twenty years; and let me tell you, Zerah, I've got hard to it and don't care a snap for it." And he suited the action to the word, with an insolence of expression and manner that would have made the woman blaze forth into fury at any other time. Now she passed his rudeness with disregard.

"Pasco!" she said in metallic tones, "there has been a load o' lead crushing down my heart. I'll shake it off and

run it into bullets against you now, and every word shall be
a bullet. Now, before Kitty, I will say what I have had
on my mind. It is you who have lied. I have known for
some time what you were thinking of. I've seen you
hovering like a hawk, and the moment I was gone—had
crossed the water—you dropped. You durstn't do it whilst
I was here. You feared me because I feared God. There's
no bigger coward on earth than the man who fears his
fellow because that fellow has God before his eyes. No
sooner was I out of the way than you at once seized the
chance offered; and I—I had gone with all my little lay-by
to get you out of your difficulties and prevent you doing
what I feared was in your intent. You'd never spoke a
word to me of that purpose of yourn, you durst not do it;
but I saw it formin' in you; I saw it, looking into your eyes,
just as you may see the sediment settlin' in dirty water.
When I was out of the way, then you thought you could do
it. You took Kitty away—who was but just home from
the moor, and all for no reason save that you didn't want
any witness. Then you left her with the cart and hoss at
Ash's linhay in Furze Park, and came back here to carry
out your purpose. So far I can see. Then my sight
becomes thick, a mist is over my eyes, and all the rest is
doubtful. What happened when you came back here—
what passed between you and Jason—what became of my
brother? All that I know not—but know I must and
will."

Pasco's face grew more sullen, and his demeanour dogged
to defiance. He could not look his wife in the face, he

kept his eyes on the ground, and with his boot scratched the floor in fantastic figures.

"I can see all that passes in your heart," pursued Zerah. "It's like as if I were outside a window, and see'd shadows on the blind as this and that went by and this and that rose up or sat down. Now the folk begin to talk and to suspect you, and say how that you insured for a big sum, and when the goods weren't paid for, burnt 'em all to secure the insurance; then you try and throw the suspicion off on to Kitty or Jason, or both together. It is like you, you black coward. But it shall not be. I will stand betwixt you and Kitty, and no harm from you shall hurt her. What I and Kitty want to know is—What has become of Jason? Where is he? If you will not answer, we will work out the answer for our own selves—she with the heable (fork), I with the phisgie (pick). We have strong arms, and we will ourselves root about in the ruins, till we learn something to satisfy our minds."

"I don't know how you've the face to talk to me like this, Zerah," said Pasco surlily. "I've come into something like four thousand pounds through my uncle, and there'll be another thousand and more from the insurance. On five thousand pounds—Lord! I'm a Christian and a gentleman."

"Bank-notes won't plaster sore consciences," retorted Zerah. "You think money is everything, and no matter how it be come by. So it has ever been with you."

"Am I like to be a villain," queried Pasco in exaspera-tion, "when I knew my uncle was worth a pot o' coin that was sure to come to me?"

"You did not know he was dead."

"I knew he was sickening and worn out. A man of means don't do criminal acts; that's the perquisite of beggars and labouring men."

"I do not ask for excuses and evasions. I ask—where is my brother?" persisted Zerah.

At that moment the door was thrown open, a hand was thrust in, waving a paper, and a voice shouted—

"There you be, Pasco Pepperill. I've got my warranty. I said I would, and I'm the man o' my word. I went full gallop up to Squire Carew. None can stand agin me."

Pepperill went to the door, saw the back of Mr. Pooke as he walked away, and the faces of a number of workmen with pick and crowbar and shovel, backed by a crowd of all descriptions of persons from the village and neighbourhood.

He hesitated for some moments. He stood irresolute, holding the door-posts and working his nails at the paint, picking it off in flakes. His heart turned sick within him. If the heaps of cinders were thrown back, then surely the remains of Jason Quarm would be discovered, and with the discovery there would ensue an inquest, and much unpleasantness if not danger to himself. With low cunning he resolved to make the best of the inevitable. He shouted to his wife—

"Zerah! bring out cider for the good fellows. They are working for us, as you know. If you have saffron cake, out with that too. I daresay I shall find a shilling apiece as well."

He went behind Pooke, slapped him on the back, and said boisterously—

"Well done, old man! That is what I wanted. If a thing has to be executed, let all be above-board and legal. That's my doctrine. I don't like no hole-and-corner proceedings. Meddlin' wi'out authority makes the end a botch. If you hadn't begun, I would have done it myself."

In the house Zerah restrained Kitty with one hand and closed the door with the other. The woman was labouring for breath, so great was her excitement. Her face was now flushed, then became wan as death.

"Kitty, my darling," she said, "I reckon I've been hard and exactin' in the past. The old pass'n were right, though I wouldn't believe him, and said he was insultin' of me to say it. 'Twas love, he told, as you wanted, and I didn't give it you. Love, the very air of heaven, wi'out which the little maid couldn't thrive. I wi'held it from you—so he told—and I shut my ears and hardened my heart. But in the end he were right. When I found out what had been done, then it broke me down. I cannot respect and love *him* no longer. I tried my best when he was foolish and unfortunate. But now he's guilty, I cannot—I cannot, and then all my love turns to you."

Kitty threw herself into her aunt's arms and sobbed.

"There's no time now for tears," said Zerah, with a gulp in her throat. "We cannot tell what is coming on us. It may be that the remains of your poor father will be found. If so, then—" Zerah shivered as if frost-smitten. "God bless us! It will be too horrible—to live under the same

roof, to eat at the same table, to see the face, hear the
voice of the man—" She was unable to conclude her
sentence. After a long pause and a hug of Kitty, she
continued: " I cannot say how it all came about. Bad as
he may be, I hardly think he did it of purpose. 'Twas
some accident. I don't mean the burning the stores—but
of your father. No; he was not so bad as that, please
God! I hope, I trust not! Now, Kitty, you and I must
make up our minds to whatever happens. And I reckon
there is but one thing us can do."

" What is that, dear auntie?"

" Hold our tongues."

After a long pause, whilst the girl clung to her, she
added, " No good can come of us speaking what we know,
and what we fancy. It can but heap up a great pile of
misery and shame. If it comes to an inquiry in court—
that's another matter. They won't call on me, as I am
Pasco's wife, but they will on you, and you must up and
speak the truth at any cost. But if there be no such
inquiry, then hold your tongue, as I will mine. The mischief, so far, has come from what we have said. We can
do no good; we may make the affair worse for ourselves if
we talk. Leave him in the hands of God, to do wi' him as
He wills."

Kate kissed her aunt and promised silence.

Then both went forth, and reached the crowd about the
ruins and piles of ashes, as Pepperill was saying in a loud
tone, " I don't say you won't find bones. I believe now I
had a pile, but all mutton and beef bones."

"Why, what were you doing wi' bones?" asked Pooke.

"Collecting of 'em for dressing," answered Pepperill promptly. "I've been in the hide line some while, and lately I took a fancy to bones also; but I didn't do much, just begun on it, so to speak—all ox and sheep bones—nothing else. Pound bones up wi' a hammer, they're fine for turnips. Jason put me up to speculating in bones."

The mass of crumbling wall, charred beam, and cinder was speedily attacked by the workmen under the direction of the constable, who had much difficulty in keeping the curious at a distance; men, women, and children were eager to assist with their hands, or advise with their tongues. They ran into danger by approaching tottering walls. They trampled down the ashes; they got in the way of the workmen; and occasionally a scream and an objurgation was the result of a labourer casting his shovelful of cinders in the face of an inquisitive spectator who got in his way. Mr. Pooke protested and stormed, but with little avail; all were too interested to attend to his orders, and he was without assistants to enforce them.

Pepperill bustled about, vociferating, driving spectators back, encouraging workmen, running after cakes and cider, and making the confusion greater. Kate sat on a fallen beam, chin in hand, watching intently every spade as it turned the ashes, wincing at every pick driven into the cinder heaps. The tears were trickling down her cheeks.

Then Walter Bramber, who had just arrived, went up to Farmer Pooke and asked leave to run a cord across from one rail to another, and volunteered with the assistance of

Noah Flood and John Pooke to keep the people from interference.

"Why should they be kept back? Don't they want to find what has become of Mr. Quarm every whit as much as me? Let 'em come on," shouted Pepperill.

But the constable saw the advantage of the proposal, and gave the order. In ten minutes the scene of the conflagration was freed from sightseers, who were confined at a distance.

Then Bramber went to Kitty and said in a low tone, "You do not think it is hopeless, I trust?"

"I do not know what to think," she answered.

"Is it true what I have heard, that your uncle returned here after dark and left you at the top of the hill?"

Kate did not answer.

"That is what is said. Jan Pooke told me he had heard it from your own lips."

She continued silent.

"I should like to know, Kitty, the truth in this matter."

"I can say nothing," she answered, and hung her head lower.

Bramber was surprised, but he had not time to expend in conversation: he had undertaken to keep off the crowd, and some were diving under the rope, others attempting to stride over it.

An hour was expended in turning about the refuse. All the coal had been consumed, but, singularly and inexplicably, not all the fleeces. Bundles of wool were found—not many, indeed, but some, singed, not consumed, which, when exposed, exhaled a sickening odour. The dangerous portions of tottering walls had been thrown down, the slate flooring exposed. Not a trace of Jason Quarm could be found.

Pasco, who had been nervous, watching all the operations of the excavators in deadly fear of a revelation of the charred remains of his brother-in-law, breathed freely, recovered all his audacity and boisterousness.

"I said as much, but none believed me. Jason is gone; he was not the man to sit quiet in a fire. How the fire came about is a question we won't go into too close."

"The bones you spoke of," said Pooke, "we ha'n't come on them. They've been consumed—perhaps poor Quarm as well. The fire must have been deadly hot."

"It didn't burn those fleeces," answered Pasco triumphantly. "I'll tell you what; Jason made off for reasons well known to himself. If we don't hear of him again, I sha'n't wonder; but burned here he certainly was not, as any fool can see. He was not the man to let himself burn. Cripple though he was, he could hop out of danger."

Pasco turned to Bramber. "What is that you have been saying to the parson about hearing Mr. Quarm and his daughter argyfying at my door the night of the fire?"

Walter Bramber was taken aback.

"Yes, you said you had heard them in hot dispute."

"I said," answered Bramber in surprise and indignation, "something very different from that. I said "—

His hand was caught by Kate, who looked pleadingly into his face.

"A word alone."

"What is it, Kitty?"

"Say nothing to anyone of what you saw and heard that night."

CHAPTER XLIV

THE mystery of the disappearance of Jason Quarm was not cleared up; on the contrary, it had become more profound. The excavation of the ruins had revealed nothing. It had disclosed no remains of the lost man, and opinions were divided. Some contended that the intense heat of the mass of coals, a heat which had split the flooring slates and burnt the soil beneath them to the depth of six inches, reddening it like brick, that this heat had completely consumed the unhappy man. On the other hand, others asked, How could that be? Some of the wool was scorched, not burnt; a man would make his way from fire; he had eyes and arms, and though Quarm was crippled, yet he could extricate himself from danger, or at all events use his powerful lungs so as to call for help. Moreover, Quarm wore brass buttons. Even if his body had been resolved to ashes, the molten buttons would be found; but no metal of any sort had been discovered on the floor.

To this responded the first: If Quarm were not burnt, how was it that he had not put in an appearance? His

74

bundle of clothes was found in the cart.   If he had escaped, he would surely either have made known his escape, or have gone off with his parcel of necessaries. Some hinted that, finding the Cellars locked, he had made his way into the warehouse, there to spend the night, and had gone to sleep with his pipe alight, and the pipe had set fire to combustibles in the place.   But then, supposing this, why was his body not found if he had been smothered by smoke? and if he had escaped, why had he not gone off with donkey, and cart, and bundle?   There was the puzzle.

Others hinted that Pasco Pepperill was the gainer by the fire, and that he had had a finger in setting the stores alight.   It was suspicious that he had sent away his wife, and had gone away with his niece just before the conflagration broke out.   There was an ugly rumour afloat, that he had returned secretly to the Cellars, and had there met and quarrelled with his brother-in-law.   This rumour was constructed out of the reported admission of Kate, and something, it was believed, that the schoolmaster had said. But neither of these, on being interrogated by the inquisitive, would say a word.   The schoolmaster, with the cheek of a stuck-up creature, had answered all inquiries with the question, "Who has authorised you to catechise me?   If the matter is brought into court, I will say what little I know on oath before the magistrate.   I will say nothing to self-constituted inquisitors."

Whenever this answer of the schoolmaster was repeated, and it was so a hundred times in the course of a week, it

never failed to elicit an indignant remark, generally couched
thus: "Them schoolmasters want setting down. They're
owdacious cocky monkeys. But they're a low lot — they
must be taught their place, which is under our heels. They
gives theirselves airs, as if they was parsons and knew
everything, but they lives on our voluntary subscriptions,
and unless they come to eat humble-pie, we'll withdraw our
farthing-in-the-pound rate. 'Tisn't for our pleasure or profit
they exist, but just because of a fad o' the pass'n. Mr.
Puddicombe was the man for us. Him we could respect.
And now they sez that Mr. Puddicombe is compoging a
Tee-dum which will cut out even Jackson."

The minds and hearts of Kitty and her aunt were
sensibly relieved. The girl had watched the exploration of
the cinder heaps with quivering nerves and brooding fear.
What might not each spade disclose? Into what an object
of horror might not her poor father be reduced? But, as
the floor of the warehouse was cleared, and every mass of
ash turned over, and nothing revealed, her heart swelled,
and the blood began again to pulsate in her arteries. She
covered her face with her hands, and lifted her heart half
in thanksgiving and half in prayer. And yet, what had
become of him? How was it that, if he were alive, he had
given no signs of life?

It was ascertained that Jason Quarm had not crossed the
estuary, either by the bridge or by boat, at Shaldon. It was
inconceivable that he had traced the creek up to its head,
below Newton Abbot, to cross the water there, as there was
no path along the water-side, and he must have come into

the road and made such a circuit as was not possible for a
man in his crippled condition.

At one moment Kitty was sanguine, at the next her
spirits fell. It was to be hoped—nay, believed—that he
had not perished in the fire; but was it not possible—nay,
probable—that he had died by some other means, that he
may have fallen into the mud, and been smothered therein?
That mud would swallow up the man that sank in it and
never restore him again. If he had come by his end thus,
had he fallen in, or had he been cast in?

Again, with a chill, as if pierced by an icicle, came the
thought of her uncle. Undoubtedly, he could explain all if
he chose. He had returned to the Cellars and found her
father there. The altercation which Walter had imperfectly
heard must have taken place between her father and her
uncle. It could not have occurred at that time, in that
place, between any others. Her father had passed by the
road as the cart entered the linhay, her uncle had gone
home immediately after. Therefore, these two had met at
the Cellars. What had been the occasion of the quarrel?
and what the result of that quarrel? The result was the
disappearance of her father. How had he disappeared?
That, she felt convinced, her uncle could answer, and he
alone. But for motives which she dared not investigate, he
remained silent; nay, worse, he endeavoured, by denial of
his having returned to the Cellars, to cast the suspicion of
having fired the storehouse from himself on other shoulders.
These questions turned and twisted in Kitty's brain without
rest. They occupied her by day, they tortured her by

night. She did not venture to express them to her aunt. She knew that the same thoughts, the same questions, were working in her mind; and she knew also that her aunt could not endure their discussion. Meanwhile, the work of the house must be carried on, and Mrs. Pepperill called in the assistance of Mrs. Redmore. With their preoccupied minds, neither she nor Kitty was capable of doing all that had been done as in days gone by.

Pasco grumbled at the introduction of this woman into his house—the wife of the wretch who had set fire to the rick of Farmer Pooke, and who had escaped pursuit. But Mrs. Pepperill did not yield. There were no other women disengaged in Coombe, and of girls she would have none to break dishes, and throw away spoons, and melt the blades out of the handles of knives.

Pasco acquiesced, with a growl, and a malicious look at Kate, and a mutter that some folk were mighty fond of incendiaries and their belongings, backing them up, helping them to escape, providing for their families; to which neither Kate nor her aunt made reply.

Pasco found that he was not comfortable at home; his wife would not unbend, and Kate kept out of his way. To his boisterous mirth, to his boastfulness, they made no response; when he stormed, they withdrew. He was uneasy in himself, suspicious of what men said of him, and alarmed when he heard from his lawyer, Mr. Squire, that the insurance company refused to pay the sum for which he had insured. Society, distraction, were necessary for him. As he could find none at home, he wandered to the village tavern, the Lamb and Flag, to seek both there.

The first occasion was the evening of the practice of the village orchestra, and it was attended by every member of the same, not only because all desired to say something relative to the matter exercising all minds, but also because the score of a new Te Deum had been placed before them, the composition of the ex-schoolmaster. Puddicombe in F was to be rehearsed by the instruments before the vocalists were called in. Puddicombe in F was expected to be a huge success, and to make Puddicombe known through the wide world of music, and to render Coombe-in-Teignhead famous in after generations, just as Exeter was known as the place which had produced Mr. Jackson, who had won such a fame with his Te Deum.

Each instrumentalist had his separate sheet of music, and each devoted himself to his score with seriousness.

Puddicombe in F began with a movement slow and stately, with all the harmonies in thirds and fifths, and a solemn tum-tum bass. Then, precipitately, it transformed itself into something headed *Fugg.* If it had been entitled *fugue*, no one would have understood what was meant. But "fugg" signified that the instruments were to perform a sort of musical leap-frog, to go higgledy-piggledy, one after the other, like children tumbling out of school, with the master behind them threatening to whack the hindermost.

And, verily, never was a fugue more of a higgledy-piggledy devil-take-the-hindermost character than this one of Puddi-

combe in F, never such a caterwauling of cats that could
surpass it in discords, with random gruntings in and out
of the violoncello.

A villager, standing breathless outside, listening, ventured
to say to the landlord, who was smoking complacently at
his door, "There don't seem to be much tune in it."

"No; but there's tremendous noise."

The landlord drew whiffs, blew out the smoke in a long
column, and said, smiling, "Wait till we come to the *largo
molto tranquillo con affettuoso caprizio*."

"What's that?" asked the bumpkin, in an awestruck
tone.

"It's something writ on the music by the hand of Mr.
Puddicombe. The Lord knows what it means!"

The hubbub of the "fugg" came to an end, and the
instruments paused, drew a sort of sigh, and, with stately
tread, marched in unison *largo molto tranquillo con affettuoso
caprizio*, and stalked through it to the end.

"There's tune there now, and be blowed," said the landlord triumphantly.

"It's the tune of 'Kitty Alone and I,'" retorted the
irreverent countryman, and he began to sing—

> "'There was a frog lived in a well,
>   Crock-a-mydaisy, Kitty alone;
> And a merry mouse lived in a mill,
>   Kitty alone and I.'"

The instruments behind the lighted window-curtains were
hushed. They had heard the rustic song.

"It is that, ain't it?" pursued the man. "I'll sing another verse, and make sure—

   "'So here's an end to the lovers three,
      Crock-a-mydaisy, Kitty alone,
     The Rat, the Mouse, and the little Frogee,
      Kitty alone and I.'"

Within, the instrumentalists looked at each other. None spoke for a minute, and then the 'cello said, in a deep voice, as from a tomb, "Puddicombe han't riz to the theme. He's forgot and worked in that frog and mouse tune. Not but what it's a good 'un, only unsootable."

"It's easy set right," observed the first violin. "If you'll wait, brothers, I'll clap on my hat and run up to his house, and get him to titch it up a bit, and git the Kitty tune out of it altogether. The fugg was famous."

"Yes," said the second violin; "it's only to stir it about a bit and shuffle as you do cards. Cut along with all your legs."

At that moment Pasco Pepperill came up, puffing, looking about him half suspiciously, half defiantly. "How are ye, gents?" said he. "What! practising? I don't mind if I sit a bit and listen to you. I'm fond of music, especially sacred music, as I'm churchwarden."

CHAPTER XLV

DAYLIGHT

THE musicians looked at each other. They could hardly continue to practise Puddicombe in F till the little awkwardness of the passage *largo molto con affettuoso caprizio* was set to rights. It would be half an hour before this was done. Meanwhile, the orchestra might as well work their tongues as well as their arms and fingers, and blow questions and puff opinions in place of musical notes. They had assembled that evening with a double intent: the excuse for their meeting was the rehearsal; the real object, the airing of their views on the fire at the Cellars, its probable origin, and what had become of Jason Quarm.

For the gathering of information on such matters, what was more fortunate than the presence in their midst of Pasco Pepperill, the man of all others best qualified to give information relative to the matters troubling all hearts? It was true that a good many—the bassoon and the ophicleide among the orchestra—entertained grave views relative to the conduct of Pepperill. Well! there the man was. They might prove him with keen questions, catch him off his guard with sly hits, entangle him in a net of incautious admissions into which they had lured him, and then sit in judgment on him and the whole case, after he had withdrawn.

"Gents and neighbours, and friends all," said Pasco, seating himself, "as churchwarden, my place is among you, and allow me to stand treat of rum and water all round— no, better than that, a grand bowl of punch, and we'll spoon it out with our good host's whalebone ladle, and the Queen Anne shilling in the bottom. Landlord, don't spare the rum; thanks to my uncle, I'm a man of means, and can pay my way."

Marvellous as a solvent is punch. The mere mention of a bowl began to melt and break up prejudice and fixed opinions. The bassoon had been persistent in insisting on the criminality of Pepperill; he had urged every point against him, he had turned aside every argument that tended to exonerate him. As a man of strict integrity, he was now placed in a difficult position. Either he must hold to his opinion, rise, bow stiffly, and decline to drink out of the bowl, to wet his lips with the generous liquor the churchwarden provided, or else his judgment must undergo modifications, then a complete *volte face*.

The popping of a cork was heard. At once the bassoon acknowledged that he had been precipitate in forming his conclusions. A waft of rum and lemons entered the room. He began to see that there were weighty considerations which had escaped him hitherto, and which undermined his convictions. Then came the clink of the ladle in the bowl, as the bowl was being brought in. The bassoon's preconceptions went down like a pack of cards. The whole room was redolent with a fragrant steam, as the great iron-stoneware bowl was planted on the table. The bassoon was converted into an ardent, enthusiastic believer in the churchwarden.

Wondrous is the power of conscience. It may lie asleep, it may remain for long inert, but a little something comes, unexpectedly touches it, and it springs up to full energy, and resolves amidst much self-reproach to make amends for the past. So was it in the interior of the bassoon. The sniff of punch was to his conscience what "Hey, rats!" is to the dozing dog. It was alive, it was stinging him, it had brought him metaphorically in penitence to his knees before Pasco Pepperill. He could not think, say, show himself, sufficiently convinced that that man who provided and paid for the punch was the embodiment of all virtues, with a character unstained as is the lily. He trampled on his own base self, he spurned at it, for having for a while thought evil of so admirable a man.

"Peter Squance bain't here. 'Tis a pity—our first fiddle," said the second violin. "He'll be mazed when he comes back with the *molto largo*, and finds the punch all gone."

"Gone?" exclaimed Pepperill. "Not a bit of it. When this bowl is done, we will have another."

Mr. Pepperill stood up and stirred the steaming sea before him, in which floated yellow islets of lemon. All eyes were on the bowl, all nostrils were dilated and sniffing, all mouths watering.

Pasco filled each glass, and then ensued a nodding all

round; eyes were turned up, lips smacked, and the precious
liquor allowed to trickle down the throats in thin rills over
the tongue.

Presently the clarionet put down his glass and said, "It
was a lucky job, Pasco, that your rick o' straw escaped
t'other night."

"Ay, 'twas a first-rate chance," said the landlord, who
had come and remained to taste his own brew and hear
encomiums on it.

"You see the wind was t'other way," said the 'cello.

"And 'twasn't insured," added the clarionet.

All the rest looked round, and frowned, and reared
their chins. The clarionet shrank together. What had he
said? Something stupid or uncivil? He was too dull to
see where his error lay.

"That had nothing to do with it. 'Twas water chucked
over it as saved it," threw in the bassoon, flying to the rescue.

"My straw rick suffered more from well-intentioned
assistants than from anything else," said Pepperill. "The
wind was direct away from it, and so it couldn't hurt."

"It was coorious, though, the fire taking place when
everyone was away from home," said the clarionet.

Again all looked indignantly at him. That instrument
had a way of always sounding out of key.

"There was nothing coorious at all in it," answered the
churchwarden, with promptitude. "It was just because
everyone was away that the fire got the upper hand."

"There's something in that," said the hautboy.

"There is everything," answered Pasco. "If I or my

wife had been at the Cellars, we would have speedily called help and had the fire extinguished before it could take hold. No one was there, so it was allowed freedom to get the mastery, and then, no one could do nothing."

"That's true," said the second violin.

"It's true," said the rest of the instruments in unison, looking into each other's faces; "it couldn't be truer."

"You don't happen to know how the fire came about?" asked the clarionet.

"I don't *know*," answered the churchwarden.

"You don't know," repeated the violoncello, "but you guess."

"I have my ideas," observed Pasco. "Gents! let me fill your glasses again."

"And if I might make so bold to ask?" pursued the clarionet.

"My mouth is shut," answered Pasco. "I don't want to hurt nobody, least of all a relation. Just fancy, gents all! the insurance company have refused payment."

"You don't say so! Well! what is the world coming to? But it all stands in prophecy, in the Book o' Dan'l," said the hautboy.

"It is one of them beasts in Revelation!" said the second fiddle. "The question only is which."

"But," pursued Pepperill, "I've set my solicitor at 'em. He'll make 'em dance a Halantow."

"Very glad to hear it," said the bassoon. "I drink to his and your success."

"We're going to institute proceedings," continued Pasco.

"What is proceedings?" asked the clarionet under his hand of the hautboy.

"It's a sort of blister o' Spanish fly," was the answer, also in confidence.

"Then it will make 'em dance, no mistake," said the clarionet. "Do you think, churchwarden, it will draw?"

"Draw?" Pasco rubbed his hands and looked round. "It'll draw getting on for fifteen hundred pound. If that bain't drawin', show me what is!"

This announcement produced a great effect.

"To go back to the p'int," said the clarionet. "It would be a comfort to us all if you'd give us your ideas on the matter of the fire. You see, we're all abroad."

"I wouldn't hurt nobody — not a fly. I was always tender-hearted," said Pasco. "Besides, you'd talk."

"We are all friends," urged the bassoon. "You see, coals don't as a rule set alight to themselves, nor wool, nor hides neither."

"That's what I've said all along," observed the second fiddle. "Someone must ha' done it. The question is— who?"

"I'll have another thimbleful of punch," said the bass viol. "It's uncommon good, and does credit to all parties—

'Come let's drink, and drown all sorrow,
For perchance we may not—
For perchance we may not meet here to-morrow.'"

Then the hautboy trolled out—

"'He that goes to bed, goes to bed sober
Falls as the leaves does—
Falls as the leaves does—in October.'"

"Someone must ha' done it," observed the clarionet.

"Of course some one did," said Pepperill, "and when folk begin yarnin' lies, you ain't got to go far to find the evil-doer."

"That's true," was the chorus.

"And no one was at the Cellars at the time but one or two persons," said the clarionet.

"One was Jason Quarm," said Pasco; "and burnt he was not, as was proved by the constable."

"I don't know," said the second fiddle. "The fire was so tremendous hot, and lasted so tremendous long, it would ha' burned a fatter man nor Jason Quarm."

"Jason's not burnt. He's runned away."

"Runned away?"

"Yes," pursued Pasco; "'cos he didn't want to have to give evidence as to what he knew."

"What wor that?"

"He comed to the Cellars, and found someone there doin' of the wickedness, and he runned away so as not to have to say what he didn't want to be forced to say."

"What was that?"

"It's not for me to speak!"

"Someone did it! who could ha' done it?" said the clarionet. "I thought it wor proved, if I may be so bould, that you, Mr. Churchwarden, comed back to the Cellars."

"I?" exclaimed Pasco, becoming purple in the face. "It suited somebody's convenience to say so, but I was in the linhay minding the hoss, and I put it to the company— no one can be in two places at once, can they?"

"There's something in that."

" I was minding the hoss, but I sent somebody back to lock up. I name no names, and she's gone and put it on me to clear herself."

The eyebrows of all the instrumentalists went up.

" Kitty? What! Kitty Alone?"

" I name no names," said Pasco; "but I must say this to clear myself. I've borne hard words too long for the sake of sheltering she. The schoolmaster heard her father lecturing of her for what she'd done."

" But she wouldn't do it out of pure wickedness," urged the clarionet; "and what reason had she?"

" There it is," answered Pasco. "I see I'm among friends, and it won't go no farther. I'd been speaking to her rather sharp for her goings-on with young men, drawin' on Jan Pooke, then kicking him over, then Noah Flood, and same with he. Noah, poor fellow, was took cruel bad along of she—ever since Ashburton fair had a pain in the stomach; if that ain't love, show me what love is. Then she took up with that schoolmaster chap, and when I said I wouldn't have it, and I wasn't going to have the family disgraced wi' bringing schoolmasters into it, she cut rusty, and sulked, and I believe it were naught but spite."

" But," observed the clarionet, "the tale I was told of what the schoolmaster said wasn't quite that."

" You are right there," said Pasco. "He'd alter his tale when he found what she'd been about. As is nat'ral. I put it to the company, if you was sweetheartin', and you found your love had been up to wickedness, you wouldn't tell tales of her, but would do all you could to screen her."

" That's true," was the general opinion.

" And you think Jason see'd her, and made off?" said the bassoon.

" That explains everything," observed the violoncello.

" I begin to see daylight," remarked the hautboy.

At that moment, in rushed the first violin, waving the score above his head.

" I've got it!" he said. " Nothing easier. It wasn't no fault o' Puddicombe, he said it were our stoopidity. 'What does *largo molto con affettuoso caprizio* mean?' he asked. '*Largo molto,* turn the score upside down, *con affettuoso caprizio,* and go ahead like blazes!'"

CHAPTER XLVI

A TRIUMPH

THE fumes of the punch had been dissipated, not only from the room of the Lamb and Flag, but also from the brain of the orchestra.

The bassoon's scruples revived; he was still grateful for the punch, but resentful for the headache it had produced.

The several points brought out by the clarionet, that provoking advocate for Pasco, who asked awkward questions and propounded awkward suggestions, stood twinkling like sparks in tinder. The bassoon thought that punch, good thing though it might be, did but momentarily overflow, and did not drown, doubts. It darkened the burning questions, but did not quench them. The disappearance of Quarm was not satisfactorily explained. The coincidence of the voiding of the Cellars conveniently for the fire, was not explained. The contradiction between the statements made by the uncle and the niece was unsifted. The bassoon grunted in his bed a grunt of dissatisfaction with himself for having yielded his opinions, a grunt of resentment against Pasco for having obfuscated his clear judgment, a grunt of resolve never again to allow his opinions to give way before punch. Conscience, that capricious factor, which had pricked him in one direction last night, pricked him in another this morning.

The hautboy, also, was out of tune. On review of the events of the past night, he considered that the entry of Pasco was an unwarrantable intrusion. The rule was well known that during a practice of the orchestra no one should be admitted. Pepperill had entered uninvited, had forced himself into their society, and he must have done that for a purpose. For what purpose but to cajole, to hoodwink them?

In vain is the net spread in the sight of any bird. The hautboy was a very wideawake and watchful bird, and he saw the meshes clearly. In vain is the hook cast in clear water; and the medium was so transparent that the hautboy plainly saw the hook. He resolved to maintain an independent, observant attitude, to form his own opinion, not accept ready-made views served up to him with punch. When before had the churchwarden favoured the village orchestra with punch? Never—since Pasco had been churchwarden. Never when in a private capacity. Only when popular feeling became suspicious or hostile, did he show himself free-handed. His present liberality told against him.

The violoncello also entered into commune with himself. Was there any chance of another brew? Would another bowl of punch be produced to keep up the favourable opinion formed on the preceding evening, or would a mistrustful attitude act as a stimulant to excite greater liberality? One brew of punch was not much, it prepared the soil, a second would sow the seed, a third make it germinate, a fourth develop, and only a fifth fructify conviction in the integrity of the provider.

The words spoken by Pepperill relative to Kate had spread. The orchestra confided them to their spouses, and the wives whispered them to their intimates. There arose in Coombe-in-Teignhead two rival factions. One party contended that Pasco was guilty, the other argued that Kitty had fired the storehouse. The advantage of the latter view was that it explained what was otherwise inexplicable—the disappearance of Quarm. The story was worked into shape; it was elaborated in detail. Kitty, of a morose and vindictive nature, had been exasperated because her uncle had forbidden her engagement to the schoolmaster. Kitty had never been as other girls were. Her reserve was slyness, her bashfulness sulkiness. Her schoolfellows had disliked her. Their mothers shared the feelings of their daughters. As the proverb says, " Still waters run deep," and of the stillness of Kitty there could be no question.

The dislike entertained of Kitty had been vague and unreasonable. Now a reason was supplied, and consistency given to what had been shapeless.

It was suspicious that Kitty had volunteered the statement relative to her being left in the linhay before she had been asked questions relative to her whereabouts. Why should she have blurted this out to Jan Pooke and

Rose Ash, but for the purpose of throwing dust in their eyes?

Kitty had been unwarrantably forward in telling her tale, and the schoolmaster unwarrantably reticent relative to his experience. Why did the schoolmaster refuse to speak out what he had seen and heard at Coombe Cellars, on that eventful night. The reason was plain enough. He did not desire to compromise Kitty. But it was clear what had occurred. She had been sent back to the Cellars by her uncle, and there her malignant spirit had induced her, out of revenge, to set fire to her uncle's stores. Her father had come on her red-handed, and had rebuked her sharply. That was what the schoolmaster had overheard. Then Quarm, finding it too late to undo the mischief done by his daughter, afraid to call in neighbours to his aid, lest Kitty should be compromised, had made his escape. There were a thousand other ways by which he might get away besides crossing the Teign. No one had thought of that. Every one had considered only whether he had crossed by ferry or by bridge. There were a score of lanes at the back of Coombe by which he might get away unperceived. All attention and investigation had been devoted to the water, and every other means of evasion left unconsidered.

Thus was the case worked out against Kitty. It assumed deeper colouring when it was remembered that she had allowed Roger Redmore to escape when entrusted with the charge of him by Jan Pooke, and Jan had said that as he left Roger he could not free himself, without Kate's consent. It was noted, also, that she had, as her uncle had told, deliberately and of *malice prepense*, frustrated the efforts he made to catch the incendiary at Dart-meet.

She had, moreover, induced her father to give up his house to Jane Redmore. Birds of a feather flock together —and surely fireflies are actuated by mutual sympathy.

On the other hand, the party that held Pepperill to be guilty were not silent. Who was the gainer by the fire? Pasco, to the amount of twelve hundred pounds. Was it not certain that he had been greatly embarrassed for money? that a bill of his had just been dishonoured? Was it not just as probable that his story was false as that of Kate? Was it she who sent away Zerah across the water? Who persuaded Pasco to drive in the direction of Newton? Did not all his proceedings on that eventful evening show a deep-laid plan? And so on.

The pros and cons were thrashed and re-thrashed over the tavern table and the ale-mugs, and over the tea in private houses. Hardly any other topic occupied men's minds and women's mouths, till suddenly something happened which silenced everyone.

The insurance company had refused payment, and the solicitor of the company sent down an agent to Coombe that he might collect information which might justify them in their refusal. At once all became mum. No one knew anything, no one suspected anybody. Nothing had happened but what was natural and easily accounted for. This change was due to the fact that there is, and more than half a century ago there was, a strong *esprit de corps* in a secluded village, that resented any intrusion of a stranger into its affairs. The rural mind is naturally suspicious, and naturally mistrusts anyone not intimately known, and regards any questions asked as something to be evaded, and on no account to be answered.

When, accordingly, the agent came among the Coombe-in-Teignheadites, and busied himself in cross-examining the people, they snapped their mouths as an oyster snaps before a lobster; or they may be likened to hedgehogs that rolled themselves up and presented nothing but prickles to the inquirer intruding in their midst. Never in his life had the man come among people like these; they neither saw with their eyes, nor heard with their ears, nor thought with what they called their brains.

Pasco took no measures to protect himself. He knew his fellow-villagers well enough to be sure that they would say nothing against him.

After a week spent in unprofitable investigation, the agent retired. At once the whole place woke up. Everyone uncoiled, every mouth opened, and every brain worked again. The rival factions recommenced their warfare, and the difference in opinion became poignant.

In due course the case of Pepperill against the insurance company came off, or rather, was announced to come off.

Pepperill was full of consequence.

He had felt acutely that suspicion hung about him like a cloud which he could not dissipate. Men who had hitherto courted his society now avoided him. The rector was especially cold in demeanour towards him. The orchestra

remained divided in opinion, agreed only in desire for more
punch.   When, after church, he approached a group at the
graveyard gate that was in eager conversation, his approach
silenced the talkers and broke up the conclave.   He was
certain that he had been their topic.   Hands that had
formerly been extended to him now remained buried in
trousers-pockets.   Voices that had given him the good-day
now withheld salutations.   Customers were reluctant to deal
with him.   His appearance in the bar of the Lamb and Flag
induced a hasty rise, a payment of shot, and a departure of
all save sodden topers.   By no other means were they to
be retained save by the offer of drink at his expense.   When
he bragged, his boasts fell flat; when he joked, none laughed.

In ill-humour and uneasy, Pasco departed for Exeter.
The case, however, never got into court.   At the last
moment the Company, convinced it had no grounds to go
upon, agreed to pay.

This was a triumph for Pepperill.   He deferred his return
to Coombe for a week, that the news might be carried to
everyone there, and have time to ripen in the somewhat
sluggish brains of the natives, and produce the effect he
anticipated.

The triumph of Pepperill was more than his own individual
triumph.   When the tidings had well soaked in, then Coombe
awoke to the knowledge that the entire parish had achieved
a victory, and that over an influential, moneyed, and powerful society.   Whether Pepperill was guilty or not guilty was
immaterial.   The fact remained that a little parish like
Coombe, by its representative, Pasco, its churchwarden, had

stood up face to face with the capital of the county, represented by the insurance company, and that the latter had
cringed and acknowledged defeat without daring to measure
arms.   That was something unheard of heretofore.   If
Coombe-in-Teignhead were not proud of its doughty
champion, then it would cover itself with disgrace.   The
situation was discussed in the bar of the Lamb and Flag,
and a self-constituted committee formed to celebrate this
momentous achievement.   The rector was to be solicited
to have a special service, at which Puddicombe in F would
be performed and a sermon preached.   The rector had a
service on Saints' Day, attended only by a few old women.
Who cared for the saints?   But Pepperill—who had extorted
one thousand two hundred pounds from the insurance company—that was the sort of man to honour, and the service
in his honour would be attended by all Coombe.   The bells
should be rung.   There had been a disturbance with the
parson about the right to the belfry on the occasion of
Puddicombe's return.   The parish must assert and maintain
its right to ring the bells when it chose, and defy the rector
if he objected.

As was feared, Mr. Fielding raised objections to both the
thanksgiving service and to the peal of bells.   Thereupon
ensued another meeting in the bar.

Now Mr. Pooke, senior, came forward.   He had been
opposed to Mr. Pepperill; he had disapproved of his
conduct.   But when it came to a matter of ringing of
bells, he felt that a principle was involved.   If once the
parishioners yielded that point, they might as well yield

everything, and be priest-ridden. There were two church-wardens; Pasco Pepperill was one, Mr. Ash, the miller, was the other, having succeeded at Lady-Day to Whiteaway, the grocer. Let Mr. Ash insist on the bells being rung, and if the rector withheld the key, then let him authorise the blacksmith to break open the door. He, Yeoman Pooke, would back him up.

They could not force Mr. Fielding to preach a sermon, but that didn't matter; they'd have music, and have it in the road, and escort Pasco Pepperill home to the strains of Puddicombe in F.

Carried by acclamation

CHAPTER XLVII

PARTED

I F anything had been needed to clinch in Pasco Pepperill the sense of his conduct being irreproachable, the ovation on his return to Coombe-in-Teignhead would have served this purpose; but nothing was necessary after that the insurance office had thrown up the ball. The retirement of the Company from the contest, and the payment of the money for which his stores were insured, acted on his conscience as much as would a plenary papal absolution on that of a Roman Catholic.

Previous to this his conscience had given occasional twitches, now it glowed with conscious sense of righteousness. It was vexed with neither qualm nor scruple. He held his head higher, boasted louder, strutted with more consequence, and became impatient and offended at his wife's maintaining her distance. He might deceive himself, deceive the world, but he could not blind her, and this made him angry. He was slighted in his home, where he had best claims for recognition.

He was, moreover, disappointed that there was so little real enthusiasm for himself at the back of the demonstration, which was organised rather in honour of the parish than of himself. The same suspicion attended him, the same reluctance to deal with him, and the same indifference to his society.

The demonstration was destined not to pass without leaving some unpleasant consequences.

At the urgency of Farmer Pooke, Miller Ash, the second churchwarden, had forced the belfry door and admitted the ringers, and authorised them to give a peal of welcome to the returning conqueror.

Mr. Fielding was of a mild and kindly disposition, but he was a stickler in matters of discipline, and he could not suffer this high-handed conduct to pass unquestioned. Ash was cited before the archdeacon, and legal proceedings were instituted to establish the sole right of the incumbent to order when and by whom the bells should be rung. Ash was dismayed at the prospect of a suit. He attempted to fall back on Pooke, but found that Pooke was by no means inclined to find money for the defence.

Mr. Fielding was reluctant to proceed against a parishioner and a churchwarden, and a man eminently worthy, but he considered that it would be a neglect of duty not to do so. Twice had he been defied, and twice had the bells been rung on improper occasions. He was aware that his action must produce ill-feeling against himself, but he was too conscientious a man to allow this consideration to weigh with him. Nothing is easier than for a man in authority to court popularity by giving way at every point. Mr. Fielding did not desire popularity, and he did not believe that in discharging a duty he would interfere with his ministerial influence in the place.

And, in fact, Ash did not so much resent the action of the rector as the unreliability of Pooke—a man who had urged him to act, and had promised to take the responsibility on himself for such action; a man whose son was about to marry his own daughter. Ash was bitter at heart, in the first line with Pooke, and the second with Pepperill, for having occasioned this affair. If Pepperill had never insured, never had allowed his warehouse to be burnt, never had confronted the Company, this unpleasantness would not have arisen; and only in the third line did his resentment touch the rector. Moreover, Pooke was discontented and uncomfortable. He was well aware that he was morally responsible for the infraction of the belfry, but he would not admit it, lest it should cost him money. Pooke was a man ready to admit a moral obligation up to ten-and-six; not a penny beyond. He allowed that the parson was in the right to stick out for his authority, and if the law gave him command of the bell-ropes—well, he was justified in trying to obtain it. But it was Pasco Pepperill who was really to blame. He ought not to have delayed his return from Exeter. Why did he stick at that city for seven whole days after he had got what he wanted? Had he come flying home by the Atmospheric the day he received payment, there would have been no demonstration. By dawdling in Exeter, he allowed time for the organisation of a demonstration, and he did not deserve one, Heaven knew! So Pooke's self-reproach converted itself into anger against Pepperill. In the physical world all forces are correlated, and it is so in the world of feeling. Love becomes hate, and joy turns into grief, and, as we have seen, compunction glances away from self and converts itself into a sting aimed at another.

Kitty's position in the place became one full of discomfort. Not only was she regarded as guilty of the fire by one body of the inhabitants, but she had given offence to others by her engagement to the schoolmaster.

Walter Bramber was not merely a pleasant-looking man, but a good-looking one as well, and several young and middle-aged women in the place had set their caps at him.

One of these was the distorted milliner, designed for him by his landlady, and encouraged by her in hopes of exchanging her condition of maid without a home for wife in the schoolhouse. This person went about to all the farmhouses making garments for the farmers' wives and daughters, and was able, without allowing it to transpire that she had aspired to Bramber, to stir up a good deal of ill-feeling against Kitty, who had been lucky where she had failed.

Another was a good-looking wench with a flaw in her reputation, who had hoped that the new-comer would be ignorant of her past history, and would succumb to her charms, and enable her to repair her faulty character out of the respectability of the position she would acquire.

Another, a damsel of erratic ecclesiasticism, who became

a Particular Baptist or an Anglican Churchwoman, according as desirable young men attended chapel or church.

The last was a widow on a nice income of her own, some twenty years Bramber's senior, who had made up her mind to marry again, and marry a young man.

Pasco was subjected to passive suspicions, Kate to active hostility. The art of ingeniously tormenting is one that men are too dull to acquire, and too clumsy to exercise. It is an art easily exercised and rapidly perfected by women. In a hundred ways Kate was annoyed by those of her own sex in Coombe; and these were ways skilfully contrived to excite the maximum of pain. She endeavoured to keep entirely to herself, but this was beyond her power. No mosquito curtains have been contrived which a person can draw about himself as a protection against malignant and poisonous tongues.

Without malicious interest — on the contrary, with the kindest desire for Kate's welfare — Rose Ash interfered and caused her the greatest distress.

Rose had set her mind on matching Kate with Noah; she by no means approved of the engagement to Walter Bramber. A girl like Kate, enjoying her friendship, might look higher, do better than throw herself away on a two-penny-ha'penny schoolmaster, of whose origin nobody knew anything; and when Rose took an idea into her head, she left no stone unturned till she had carried it out.

She visited Kate, she assured her that a union with Bramber was out of the question. There was so strong a feeling against her in the place that, were she to marry the schoolmaster, it would damage his prospects. The farmers would withdraw their subscriptions from the school, and the parents refuse to send their children to be educated there.

"Of course," said Rose, "I don't believe you burnt the warehouse, but a lot of people in the place do. Some say you did it out of spite, because your uncle wouldn't let you have the schoolmaster; others say he sent you back to set the wares alight, being too much of a coward to do it himself. I know better—but folks won't listen to me. I don't see how you can put the notion out of them but by marrying Noah. He's related to nearly everyone in the place, and if you became his wife, you see, all the relations of Noah would take your part; they'd be bound to do it. Noah is a good fellow, and he's terribly in love —got a pain under his ribs, and walks bent—all along of love. You'd best chuck over the schoolmaster and stop their mouths with Noah. There's no other way of doin' it."

"You really think that my engagement to Walter Bramber will injure him?"

"If it goes on, he may as well leave the place. It would be made too hot to hold him. You see, Kitty, the Coombites ha' never taken much to him—he bain't like Mr. Puddicombe in nothing. But they might get used to him and put up wi' him. If you go on holding him to his engagement, then — what everyone says is — he must go."

Zerah, moreover, sought to influence her niece. She

was a selfish woman, and now that she had opened her heart to Kitty, she was jealous of anyone else claiming a share in the girl. Moreover, she could not endure to live at the Cellars if left there alone with Pasco, of that she was convinced. She therefore extorted a promise from Kate not to leave her.

Kitty had become more than ever thoughtful, and was nervous and depressed in spirits. She could not clear herself of this suspicion that attached to her without incriminating her uncle, and she greatly doubted whether her word would avail against his. She could not hear anything of her father, the same mystery enveloped his fate unrelieved. She would have liked to pour her troubles into the ear of Walter, but her uncle had forbidden his coming to the house, and she would not go and seek him, observed, watched by all, and everything she did subject to misconstruction. Kate's time was more at her disposal than formerly, as Jane Redmore came in charing. This was a disadvantage to her, so far that it allowed her time to brood over her troubles and annoyances.

After Rose had gone, she went on the water side of the house and seated herself on the parapet above the rippling inflowing tide, with her head sunk on her bosom.

Presently the tears began to course down her cheeks. She had not been seated there long before the timid, feeble Jane Redmore came fluttering out to her, looking over her shoulder as she came. The woman touched her:

" I wouldn't take on so," she said. "You ain't sure Jason Quarm's dead, you know. He wasn't found, and for why?"

Kate looked at the poor woman with tear-filled eyes.

"I can't say nothin'," said Mrs. Redmore hastily. " Only—there—it makes me bad to see you cry, it do, and I reckon there's no reason."

Then she slipped back in the same wavering, timid manner to the kitchen, without another word.

But Kate's distress of mind was not due solely, as the woman believed, to her anxiety concerning the fate of her father. She had been debating in her heart whether she ought to continue her engagement with Bramber, and, perhaps, never had Kitty felt how truly she was "alone" as now, when she had satisfied herself that for his sake it were well for her to release him.

She stood up, when her purpose was formed, and walked quietly, firmly, to the Rectory. One friend she had there, ever faithful—the parson. He knew that she was innocent, he alone could appreciate her difficulties, and he would approve her determination.

She entered the study where he was at work on a sermon. He smiled, and his face brightened when he saw her, and he signed to a chair.

Kate, direct, clear, and firm in all she said and did, told the rector of her intention. She informed him of what he knew already, that a body of feeling was engaged against her, that she was incapable of establishing her innocence. That, under the circumstances, it was out of the question her holding Walter Bramber to his promise. She had, furthermore, passed her word to her aunt not to leave her. Mr. Fielding, though disappointed, saw that under the circumstances nothing could be done ; and he felt that Kate was acting honourably and in accordance with her conscience. He knew, therefore, he must not dissuade her from obedience to that inner voice. He took a more hopeful view than did she, and this he expressed.

"If things change, then no harm has been done," said Kate. "I have to say what is in my mind as made up on things as they are. Will you be so kind, sir, as to speak to Walter?"

"I see him coming in at the gate," said Mr. Fielding. "He is with me about this time every day for a Greek lesson — a bit of New Testament in the original tongue."

Kate stood up.

"Yes," said he. "You go to meet him at the mulberry tree."

The girl left quietly and composedly, as she had entered, and, crossing the lawn, came on the young man just as he reached the bench under the mulberry.

"Walter," she said, " I want a word with you. Have you a knife?"

"Yes; why?"

"Will you cut this in the mulberry bark? Mr. Fielding will not object—

'O Tree, defying time, witness bear,
That two'"—

She hesitated, slightly coloured—

'"That two friends met and parted here.'"

"What do you mean, Kitty?"

"Ask the rector—he will tell you all."

Then hastily, unable further to control herself, she passed him, and left the garden.

CHAPTER XLVIII

A SHADOW-SHAPE

KATE walked at once to the house of Mr. Puddicombe, and, without giving any reasons, announced to him that the engagement to Walter Bramber was at an end. She calculated on his publishing the fact, but she had not calculated on his inventing and promulgating reasons of his own supposition for explaining the rupture. According to him, she had formed a preference for Noah Flood, and regarded an alliance with Noah more to her advantage than one with a person of whose origin nothing was known, and whose prospects were uncertain. One of the first to hear the news was Rose Ash, and she made an excursion immediately to the house of the Floods, where Noah lived with his mother, a widow. The Floods were a well-to-do yeoman family, with land of their own. The father of Noah had died three years previous to the events recorded in this tale. Noah was the only child, and had been the idol of his mother. That he should seek a wife, she admitted, was natural. She would greatly have preferred his taking some-one of more position and means, and in greater favour than Kitty Alone, but she was accustomed to regard everything

her son did as right, and she would not offer any opposition
to what he determined on.   As Rose Ash was not to be
won, he might take Kitty; though she would have vastly
preferred Rose.   The old woman was, it is true, made
uneasy by the reports relative to Kitty and the fire at the
Cellars, but her son knew how to set her mind at rest, by
ridiculing them as idle and baseless, bred of malice or
stupidity.

Rose was really energetic on behalf of Kitty.   She did
brave battle for her, and combated every adverse opinion.
She was thoroughly resolved to forward the match between
Noah and Kate, and now that the field was cleared of the
schoolmaster, she hurried to the house of the Floods to spur
on Noah to immediate action.

The evening was already closing in, and the house of the
Floods was at some distance out of Coombe; but Rose was
impulsive, and what she did was done in impulse.   She was
generous, so far as did not interfere with her own prospects and wishes and comforts.   Mrs. Flood was her aunt,
and with her she was ever welcome.   Noah was happily at
home when Rose arrived.   She was not the girl to beat
about the bush, and she rushed at once upon the topic
uppermost in her mind.

"You must put on your hat at once, Noah, and come
with me.   I'm going to the Cellars, and going to make all
right between you and Kitty.   The time has arrived.   The
door is ajar, and you must thrust your shoulder in before
it is shut.   It's off with the schoolmaster, and must be on
with you at once."

"Noah hasn't been hisself of late," said Mrs. Flood. "I don't think he ought to be out with the dew falling heavy."

"Nonsense, Aunt Sally! it's love," said Rose. "The dew won't hurt. It's his disappointment has upset him."

"He's been off his feed terrible," said the mother; "there is a nice piece of boiled bacon I've had cold, but he don't seem to relish it."

"That's love," said Rose; "and I heard Mr. Pepperill say that Noah had a pain under his ribs."

"It's like a hot pertater lodged here," said Noah; "I can't get no rest at all from it."

"That's love also; I know it. I've had the same till Jan came to his senses."

"And I don't seem to take no interest in the farm; do I, mother?" asked Noah.

"Indeed you don't, Noah."

"That also is love," said Rose; "we'll soon put that to rights."

"I thought it was liver," observed the mother; "and that blue pill "—

"Oh, nothing of the sort," interrupted Rose. "I know all the symptoms: hot potato, distaste for biled bacon, and indifference to farm affairs—it's love; I had it all badly till Jan came round. Love turns heavy on the chest, if disappointed. That's what Noah feels under his ribs. Come on, Noah, take your hat, and we will go to the Cellars together."

Noah complied with as much alacrity as he was capable

of displaying. He was a docile youth; he had fallen in love with Kitty, partly at Rose's bidding, partly out of compunction at his conduct at the fair.

That evening had closed in rapidly. There were dense clouds overhead, so that the twilight was cut off, also all danger of dew, as Rose at once pointed out to Mrs. Flood. As, however, the mother feared her dear boy might get wet in the event of rain, Noah was induced to take a greatcoat.

The young man was shy and timid.

"You know, Rose, I treated her terrible bad at Ashburton, when I knocked away the workbox from under her arm."

"She will like you all the better for it," answered the girl. "Young maidens like a lad of spirit, and you may be sure it gave her pleasure to see you and Jan punching each other's heads. That schoolmaster! he ain't up to nothing but whacking childer with a cane. If you like, I'll try and egg him on to fight you, and then you can knock him all to pieces; and there's nothing surer for finding your way to Kitty's heart. If she's like me, she'll like to see lads fighting about her."

"You don't think, Rose, she really had anything to do wi' the fire?"

"The fire?" snapped the girl. "No more than you or I. Her uncle did it. He wanted the insurance money. That's a fine tale—that she set fire to the warehouse, because her uncle wouldn't hear of her marrying the schoolmaster—and now, of her own accord, she throws the fellow over. If she

had been so set on him, she wouldn't have done *that*. Can't
you see, Noah, or are you stupid, that her giving up Mr.
Bramber is the best answer to that story? It shows it
could not have been. And then, as to that other tale,—
that Mr. Pepperill sent her back to set the place in a blaze,
—no one who knows Kitty can believe *that*. She's not the
girl to do a wrong thing at anyone's bidding. Besides, what
good would it have been to her?"

Noah did not answer.

"You can't do better than go right up to her and ask her
to be yours—now. Everything is in your favour. Folk
talk a pass'l of nonsense and spiteful lies about her. It
makes her cruel unhappy. She's been doing little else but
cry for some days. You show her you don't mind one snap
what folks say, and you don't believe a word o' the lies
against her, and I tell you she'd jump into your arms. It's
my belief that the schoolmaster turned nasty—that he
began to show her he thought there might be something in
it, that he knew people said they'd take away their sub-
scription if he married her, and he made it so unpleasant
for Kitty that she gave him up. And now you march in
and conquer."

"I'll do so," said Noah.

"And," pursued Rose, "you must begin by making
Kitty cry; that's the preparing of the ground."

"How am I to do that?"

"Talk about her father. Ask if she has heard any news
of him."

"Why? it don't seem kind to make her cry."

"What a noodle you are, Noah! Nothing is more profitable for what you intend than to get her into a crying mood, regular soft and tender, and then pity her about her father, and so out with it when she is in tears. That's the way to win her!"

Noah mused awhile, walking by the side of Rose, in silence. After a minute he said, "What is your notion, Rose? I mean about Jason Quarm. Is he dead or not?"

"Of course he is. Burnt to ashes."

"But the ashes were not found."

"My dear Noah, you saw the fire as well as I; you know with what fury it burnt, and how it lasted three days. He was no Shadrach, Meshach, and Abednego all pounded into one."

"You really think he is dead?"

"Sure of it. Would he not have turned up and let folk know he was alive, if he had not perished Would he have allowed Kitty to go on—and not Kitty only, his sister Zerah as well—all this long time, suffering and miserable, because they believe he died a terrible death, if he could relieve their minds by a letter, or, better still, by appearing?"

Suddenly Rose started, caught her cousin by the arm, and drew back.

"What is the matter?" asked the young man.

"There is something there—moving—in the hedge."

They were in a true Devonshire lane, with the hedges high on each side, planted with trees that extended their branches overhead, almost interlocking. Through the

boughs and leaves the grey sky glimmered, and the soil in
the lane here and there showed in the light from above, but
all was indistinct and dark. A turn in the lane, and a fork
beyond the turn, lay before them, and through one of the
lanes the light of the estuary reflecting the sky made a
partial gleam, as though that lane were a tube with ground
glass at the end.

Both remained motionless and listened.

"Hark!" whispered Rose; "did you hear something?"

"I heard you speaking."

"Before I spoke—a clitter, as of a foot on stones."

"Well, what of that? This is a road, and people may
go along it, I reckon."

"Look—look!" gasped Rose, pointing down the funnel-
like lane, at the end of which was the light of the steely
water.

Rose maintained her grasp of Noah.

The young man looked in the direction indicated, and
both saw a figure in the vista, lurching as it went along, as
though lame; a thickset figure, as far as they could make
out in the uncertain light. In another moment it had
disappeared.

"Go after it!" said Rose, relaxing her hold.

"It? What do you mean?"

"That's just like Jason Quarm."

"But he's dead. You said so."

"I know he is, but that's his ghost. Run, Noah, and
force it to speak. It's walking, because it can't rest wi'out
burial."

" I won't ! " said Noah. " Go yourself."

" You are a man. It's vanished now. That's the way to the cottage he had, which Kitty gave up to the Redmores. Oh, Noah, do run ! "

" I'll do nothing o' the sort. Come on, Rose—we are going along t'other lane, thanks be. Lord, that we should ha' seen a ghost ! I shan't be able to propose. I shall be so terrible took aback."

"Nonsense, Noah ! "

" But consider—it's terrible frightening to propose right on end to a ghost's daughter."

CHAPTER XLIX

NOAH and Rose reached the Cellars just as Pasco and his family were about to seat themselves to supper. Pepperill somewhat boisterously welcomed them, and insisted on their sharing the evening meal.

"You see," said he, "it is dull here. Zerah ain't much in the way of entertainment, and Kitty be just as heavy. Stupid place this, and stupid people; I shall get away as soon as possible."

"Going to leave the Cellars, Mr. Pepperill?" asked Rose.

"I don't find this place lively enough for me, now I'm a man of independent means. I want amusement, and can get none here; society, and here no one can talk of anything but bullocks."

"I don't know that," said Noah; "there is the fire, everyone is talking of that."

Rose cast a reproachful glance at her cousin. His remark made Pasco wince, and Zerah look down into her plate.

"You see," pursued Pepperill, "having come in for a little property"—

118

"The insurance money?" asked the blundering Noah.

"My uncle's little fortune," answered Pasco hastily. "There's no occasion for me to toil and drudge like a slave selling coals, and wool, and hides, and the like; so I think I'll take a little box somewhere near Exeter, somewhere where I can amuse myself, and have agreeable neighbours."

As soon as opportunity offered, Rose drew Kate aside and said to her cheerily, "I have brought you Noah."

"Noah! Why?"

"I heard you were off with the schoolmaster."

"Yes, I am."

"Then it is high time you were on with another."

"I want no one."

"Oh, that's nonsense! You must have Noah. He's a nice fellow and has a good property; besides, he is cruel sweet on you."

"Indeed, indeed, Rose, I wish to be left alone."

"It won't do, Kate. When the circus girl goes round driving two horses, she skips off one back and on to another. You can't skip off one saddle wi'out another saddle to skip into, that ain't reason."

"I am not a circus girl."

"We all are going round and round in one ring, and then comes a fool and holds up the hoop for us to go through. Jack has been my clown, and Noah shall be yours."

"I do not wish it," said Kate hastily. "I desire only to be let alone."

"My dear, I know what is best for you. I'll call Noah."

Kate sprang up. "I have to wash up after supper with Mrs. Redmore," she said, and hastened into the kitchen.

Rose was vexed. She returned to the others, and gave Noah a sign to follow the girl; and he obeyed with his usual docility. Then Rose began to propound her scheme to the uncle and aunt, to explain Noah's prospects and dilate on his attachment for Kate. The aunt alone raised objections, which Rose combated in the most airy manner. Zerah doubted whether Kate felt any regard for Noah; Rose was positive that this would come as a matter of course, now that she was free from entanglement with Bramber.

Pepperill said he would be glad, after what had happened, to have Kate married and out of his house. Whereupon Zerah caught him up and asked his meaning.

Before he could answer, Kitty came in trembling, and, standing before Rose, asked, "What does he mean? Noah says he has seen my father."

Rose tossed her head, and cast an angry glance over Kate's shoulder at the stupid young man who was following.

"Noah is a blundering fellow," she said, "and does not know what he says. Your father! Do you think that if we had seen him we would not at once have made him come on here with us?"

"You told me "—began Noah apologetically.

"Whatever I may have said, you are too dull to understand, and you turn everything cat-in-the-pan."

Apparently satisfied, Kate prepared to go back into the kitchen, and Noah would have followed her; but she stood

in the doorway and said firmly, "No, I do not wish to
have you in the kitchen. If you persist in following, I shall
pin a dish-clout to your back. Jane Redmore wants to get
home to her little ones, the night is dark as pitch. I must
help her to clean up, and we can have no one to interfere
with us; you nearly made me break a dish with what you
said just now."

"Come here," said Rose. "You are a duffer, and don't
know how to manage"; and Noah obeyed, and seated himself in the settle. Kate shut the kitchen door.

"What was that you said about my brother Jason?"
asked Zerah.

"It was nonsense," answered Rose sharply.

"But Noah meant something, when he said he had seen
him."

"Noah is a fool : are you not, Noah?"

"I suppose you know," answered the young man
meekly.

"Tell me what it was that made Kate nigh on drop the
dish," persisted Zerah, always a resolute woman to have
her way.

"It was nought but a parcel of nonsense," said Rose
evasively.

"There must have been something," persisted Zerah.

"Well, I don't mind saying," Rose replied,—"that is, if
you will hear—but it was fancy, I reckon."

"What was fancy?"

"Thinking we saw him. I had told Noah to propose to
Kate, and to get her into proper humour for accepting, first

by making her cry, and then I told him he could make her cry by speaking in a sort of sympathising way about her father; and like an old buffle-head he went and said he had seen his ghost."

"His ghost?" exclaimed Zerah, and Pasco drew back in the settle with a scared expression on his face.

"We were coming down the road from Noah's, and before us was the fork of the lane," said Rose. "Well, then, if you will hear all, Noah and me, us thought us see'd someone in the lane as went towards Jane Redmore's cottage. The night was dark, but there was light at the end of the lane because of the Teign, which was full of the tide; and there was, sure enough, someone walking down that road. Us see'd him, whoever he was. He walked like a lapwing."

"'Twas Jones Maker, the roadman," said Pasco in a voice that was not firm. "He's lame."

"He goes on a crutch," answered Rose. "What we saw was different, was it not so, Noah?"

"Yes," assented the young man. "He walked lop o' this side like, just the same as Jason Quarm."

"'Twas Jonas Maker," persisted Pasco.

"It can't ha' been Jonas," answered Rose; "Jonas is tall, and this we saw was stout and thickset."

"Did he speak?" asked Zerah breathlessly. Pasco fidgeted in his seat.

"No, he did not; us weren't very near, and I axed Noah to run on and catch him up, and ax him questions why he walked, but he wouldn't."

"I reckon Mr. Pepperill would ha' been shy to do that," growled Noah.

Then a dead silence fell on all; and in that dead silence a sound like the tread of a man with a limp was audible, coming up the steps to the door. Next as if a hand were laid on the door-hasp, and all saw that the latch was raised, and cautiously lowered, without the door being opened. Then ensued the halting hobble down the steps again.

No one stirred. Every face was blank. Possibly one of those present would have started up and gone to the door to look forth into the black night, but at this moment Kate entered, and, going up to a crook, took down a lantern.

"Jane Redmore is going home," she said, "and she's axed me just to show her off the premises and into the lane, with a light; it's too dark to find the way at once, when one has been in the room with plenty of light."

Kate opened the lantern and looked in.

"There is a candle," she said, and proceeded to ignite it.

Rose looked at Noah, and Noah at Rose.

"I think," said the girl, "we will ask you, Kate, to show us a light on our way presently, after you have put Jane Redmore into hers."

"I will do so cheerfully," answered Kitty, and went back with the lighted lantern into the kitchen to fetch Jane. Then the two passed through the room where the rest sat, and Mrs. Redmore wished them all a good-night.

Silence ensued after the door was shut. The glitter of

the lantern was visible through the window for a moment, and then disappeared.

Pasco looked uneasily at the door. He was the first to break silence. "I wish you to know," said he, "that if you marry Kitty, Noah, you do not take a beggar. On the contrary, you take an heiress."

"How do you make that out?" asked Zerah.

"Kitty is not of my blood," said Pasco, gaining firmness, "but I have no relations of my own, and I intend to treat Kitty as my child. Noah, you marry an heiress."

"What will you give her?" asked Zerah.

"Great expectations," answered Pasco pompously.

"I don't count much on expectations," said his wife contemptuously. "Give her something down."

"I'll do better than that," said Pasco. "I'll make my will and constitute her my heir."

"That's moonshine and tall talk," scoffed Zerah.

"It is nothing of the sort," said Pasco. "Here you are, Rose and Noah, and I'll make my will before you, and you shall witness it. Then Noah will know what he takes, when he takes Kitty."

Zerah looked at her husband with surprise. This was the first intimation she had received that he intended to do anything for his niece. She did not see deep enough into his heart to read his reasons. At that moment he was alarmed and uneasy at the story of the apparition of Jason Quarm, whom he knew to be dead, and then at the mysterious tread and the raising of the hasp of the door. He was not a superstitious man, but the guilt on his soul made him subject to terrors. He thought that the spirit of the man he had brought to his death might be walking, and would trouble him, not only on account of the wrong done to him, but also to his daughter. In his mean mind Pasco hoped that by constituting Kitty heir to all he possessed, he might lay the troubled spirit of her father.

"I will do it at once," said Pepperill, opening his desk and drawing forth ink and pen and paper, and laying them on the table.

"I will show you that I understand legal forms,—I keep a solicitor of my own,—and that I am the man who can deal generously and with a free hand. I, Pasco Pepperill of Coombe Cellars, being in sound condition of mind and body "—

He wrote the words, then looked round complacently and added, "I bequeath to my niece, Kate Quarm, the sum of three thousand pounds. Three thousand pounds," repeated Pasco, looking round. "Also to my wife Zerah, two thousand pounds and my house at Coombe Cellars, and my house property at Tavistock, inherited from my uncle,"—he turned his head consequentially to look at Noah, then at Rose,—"during the term of her natural life."

"What do you mean by natural life?" asked Zerah.

"It is an expression always used," answered Pasco.

"It is nonsense," said Zerah, "If there be a natural life, there must be one which is unnatural."

"It means, plain as Scripture," replied Pasco, "that you may have my house as long as your nat'ral life lasts, and after that lie quiet in your grave, and not walk and bother people. Your right to the house is tied up to your nat'ral life. That's the meaning o' that there legal term. It stops and prevents all after unpleasantness."

"Now I understand," said Zerah. "But you need not get hot over it."

"I'm not hot, but some folk be stupid and understand nothing. Now I will proceed. After my wife's decease,—that's the legal term for death,—then all goes to my niece, or reputed niece, the aforesaid Kate Quarm. This is my last will and testament, and true act and deed. Here you see me sign it. Now then, Rose Ash, and you, Noah Flood, witness my signature. You, Zerah, cannot, because you are beneficially affected."

Mr. Pepperill had completely recovered his self-consequence and his courage. He had shown Noah that he was a man of means, a man with house property, a man of capital as well, and he had eased his conscience by making satisfaction for the wrong he had done to Kate.

As soon as Pasco had seen the young people witness his signature, he handed the will to Zerah. "There, wife, keep it."

At that moment the door was thrown open, and Kate entered, and stood by the table, with changes of expression flying over her countenance, like flaws of wind on the face of a pool.

She put down the lantern on the board.

"Why, Kitty, the light is out!" said Zerah, and opened the horn door. "Why, Kitty, where be the candle to? She's gone."

At that moment, a flare that illumined the entire room, a sheet of light, entering by door and window.

"Good heavens!" exclaimed Pasco, springing up. "My rick." Then with a scream of triumph, as he pointed with one hand to Kate, with the other to the lantern, "I told you so, now you will believe me. Caught in the act."

CHAPTER L

THE THIRD FIRE

THE light poured into the room like a flood, yellow as sunlight, and more intense in brilliancy. Kitty standing at the table had her face in shadow. Pasco opposite was as a mass of gold. The fire glittered in his eyeballs, it flashed in the new heavy gold watch-chain that he had purchased in Exeter.

"Now—now I shall be believed. Now—now the world will know how falsely I have been judged. Now—now is revealed what a viper I have nu'ssed at my hearth."

"We had best go and put out the fire," said Noah, and he went to the door, to see that no possibility existed of arresting the flames. The rick was all but enveloped as in a blazing sheet that was drawing round it to meet at the only side which was dark. Little wind blew, so that the flame poured up in one tongue.

Voices could be heard, loud shouts in the village, where the conflagration had attracted attention, and had broken up the session of the orchestra. The bassoon was braying a loud note, prolonged and hideous, to rouse such as were behind curtains, and did not observe the glare.

"How did this come about?" asked Rose, catching Kate by the arm.

"I—I cannot say. I cannot say," answered the girl addressed; "but, indeed, I am not guilty."

"Is it insured?" asked Noah.

"No, it is not insured," answered Pasco triumphantly. "I hope now you won't go and say *I* did it—and that I did it to get money out of a company."

Except the words recorded, nothing further was spoken. The little party was too dismayed at the occurrence, and at the prospect of what must spring from it, to stir, to speak. It was in vain to think of doing aught to the rick. No outbuilding was endangered. An attempt to tear down the stack would result in spreading the fire.

Then in at the door burst the constable.

"Halloo! what is the meaning of this?" he shouted. "Insured again?"

"I am not insured," answered Pepperill. "If you want to arrest the culprit—there she is."

"How came this about?" asked Pooke. "I'm not going to arrest nobody without a cause."

"There is cause enough," said Pasco. "Kitty is the person who has set fire to my rick. I have plenty of evidence for that. And now that I have, you'll all see I'm innocent—white as driven snow."

"What is the meaning of this?" asked the constable, turning Kitty about that the blaze might illumine her face. In the yellow glare it could be seen that she was deathlike in complexion, and that her eyes were wide distended in terror. She trembled, and seemed unable to stand without the support of the table.

"I'll tell you all," said Pasco majestically, "and then, perhaps, Mr. Pooke, you'll believe my word in preference to that of such as she."

"What is it?" asked Pooke. "I'll not arrest nobody without good cause shown, as satisfies my judgment. I said so before."

"Look at that lantern," said Pasco.

"Well, I sees it."

"Open it. There's no candle in it—is there? But there was—a quarter of an hour ago."

Numerous voices were now audible around the burning rick. The constable looked out, and hesitated whether to go forth and ensure order without, or to hear what had to be said within.

He saw that there was not much chance of further mischief, the intensity of the fire kept everyone at a distance.

"Go on," said he. "What have you to say against the girl?"

"She was in the kitchen with Jane Redmore. And Jane Redmore asked her to go along with she on her way home, wi' a lantern, because of the pitch darkness. Was it not so, Zerah?"

"I can't say. I wasn't in the kitchen," answered Mrs. Pepperill reluctantly.

"Was it as he says?" asked the constable, turning to Kate.

"Yes." Then suddenly, she woke out of a condition of almost stupefaction; and throwing herself on her knees before her uncle, she entreated, "Do not say that I did it!"

"I leave that to the magistrate, when he tries, and commits you to prison."

"No, no, you will not send me there!"

"I shall certainly have you tried and punished."

"Uncle! I beseech you! Let me speak to you alone. I did not do it. I must have a word with you, where no one can see, no one can hear."

"Indeed, I shall not consent. You want to induce me not to prosecute. I know what you will say. I know how you will appeal to my feelings. You know well enough what a lovin' and tender and feelin' heart I've always shown. But this won't do. It won't do. I've borne the slights and the slanders because o' the last fire, and folk cried out again' me—I did it for the insurance; and now—now I hope I'll make all believe I'm not the guilty party. They must look elsewhere. Take her in charge as an incendiary, constable. Do your duty."

"Uncle! I beseech you! For my sake, for your own, go no further in this."

"I must proceed, if only to clear myself."

"Uncle!" In her anxiety she held him. "You do not know my reasons. I pray you, I pray you on behalf of me and dear aunt, as well as yourself—some terrible thing will happen otherwise!"

"I'll look to that—that no more terrible things happen. Now, constable, she's threatenin' to burn the house down over my head, to burn me and my missus in our beds. You heard her. You all heard her threaten us. I call you to witness."

"I will do no harm to anyone. I entreat a word, a word in private," urged Kate.

"I'll have no word in private," said Pepperill. "What you have to say, say out; lies, lies all it will be," he added.

"I cannot say it before all. I must speak it in your ear."

"I won't listen to nothing," said Pepperill.

"And I," said Pooke, "I won't allow of no tamperin' wi' justice, no persuadin' not to prosecute. We've had enough of these little games here. This is the third fire, and we'll have someone punished for this if I can manage it."

"You do not know what you are doing, uncle," gasped Kitty, staggering to her feet.

"I reckon I know pretty well," he answered coldly.

"You do not. You will bitterly, bitterly rue it. Do not rush on what must happen, and then tear yourself in grief and dismay that you did not listen to me."

"Listen how she threatens. Tell'e what, Mr. Pooke, there'll be no safety for none i' the parish so long as she's at large. Silence, Kitty! Neither the constable nor I will hear another word but what concerns this fire, and what will serve to convict you."

"Did you go with the lantern all along wi' Jane Redmore?" asked Pooke.

Kate recovered her composure, and, with a despairing action of the hands, dashed the tears from her eyes.

"Answer me," said Pooke; "no prevarication."

" I went out with Jane."

" Did you accompany her home?"

" No, only a little way."

" How far?"

" To the gate."

" What! not into the lane even?"

" No."

" How long was she absent?" asked Pooke.

"Long enough for me to draw up a document," said Pepperill. "What should you say, Zerah? Half an hour?"

Zerah was in no condition to answer.

"And why did you not go on with Jane Redmore?" asked the constable of Kitty.

"Because—I cannot say."

"Oh, you cannot say? Mind, what you speak now may be used again' you at your trial. I'm bound to tell you that, and you ain't obliged to answer. Nevertheless, if you can give a reasonable account of yourself, I'm not called on to think you guilty, and arrest you. What was you a-doing of yourself all that half an hour, when you wasn't with Jane Redmore, a-seeing of her home?"

He paused for an answer, and received none.

"Am I to understand you won't say? You ain't forced to do so, you know."

" I had rather not say," replied Kate in a low voice.

" I suppose there was a candle in the lantern when you went out?"

" Yes."

" Was it burnt out?" Pooke looked into the socket in

the lantern. "No," he said; "it has illicitly been removed. There is no guttering of grease. How do you account for that?"

Kate made no answer.

"We know very well how your rick was fired," said Pepperill. "It seems to me, Mr. Pooke, that mine was set alight to in much the same way."

"How do you account for the candle being gone?" asked the constable.

Again no answer.

"Now, look here," said he. "You're a little maid, and I don't want to deal hard with you. If you can give me an explanation of your conduct as will satisfy, why, I'll not proceed to extremities. But I must say that things look ugly. If you was innocent, you could say so."

"I am innocent."

"Then how came the rick to be fired?"

Kate made no reply. She was trembling, and nervously plucking at her light shawl, tearing away and unravelling the fringe.

"You alone had the lantern. It wasn't Mrs. Redmore now—eh?—or her husband?"

"Oh no, no!" replied Kate eagerly. "She had nothing to do with it. She had gone away along the lane, some time before"— She halted.

"Oh! you know how the fire arose?"

Kate gave no reply.

"I'm afraid it's a bad case, and I must do my duty, and convey you to the lock-up."

"Oh, aunt!" cried the girl, turning towards Zerah, who stood cowed, speechless, in the background. "Oh, aunt! let me speak with you alone."

"No! it is of no use," said Pasco, stepping between the girl and his wife. "Nothin' that she can say to Zerah will avail, and certainly nothin' that Zerah can say will persuade me. Remove her at once."

The constable laid his hand on Kate's shoulder.

"One question more. Mind, I caution you not to answer unless you choose. If Mrs. Redmore was not with you, she had gone on. Were you alone, Kitty, in the stack-yard after she left; and how was it you were there so long? Say, was there anyone with you?"

"Aunt, let me speak to you!" in a despairing cry.

Zerah made a movement towards her niece, but Pepperill intercepted her, and, catching her by the shoulders, rudely thrust her back. "You shall not speak with her." Then, turning his head, with a coarse laugh, "So, someone with her! The schoolmaster, I suppose. She had given him up, and was inclined to take him on again. Women change like weathercocks."

"Mr. Bramber was not there," said Kate, a flush mantling her brow.

"Then who was it?"

Dead silence.

"Come, Kate Quarm, with me. I must do my duty," said the constable.

"Stay!" said the rector, who had entered unperceived. "Trust her with me. I solemnly promise that I will keep her secure. Let her go with me to the parsonage, and do not, in pity, take the frightened, innocent child "—

"Innocent?" in a mocking tone from Pasco.

"Innocent child," repeated the rector, with his eye on Pepperill, who dropped his at once. "Mr. Pooke, rely on me to produce her when you require. In pity, do not frighten her; she may be able easily to clear herself. That she is innocent, I stake my word. Trust her to me."

The constable hesitated. The lock-up was in a bad condition. It had not been occupied for years, and had been turned into a poultry-house.

"Come, Kitty," said the rector. "I have made myself answerable for you. And I am proud to do so."

CHAPTER LI

NOT a word on that evening would the old rector allow himself to speak to Kitty relative to the fire, nor would he suffer her to speak about it. He saw that she was in a condition of nervous excitability, and that she must be tranquillised. But, indeed, she made hardly an attempt to speak about the rick, and how it was set on fire ; and directly the rector put up his hand to indicate that the topic was taboo, she submitted with a sense of relief.

Mr. Fielding had a kind, motherly housekeeper, with tact, and, at a word from him, she understood how that Kate was to be treated. The rector was, indeed, alarmed lest the fright and mental excitement he found the girl labouring under might throw her into fever. He knew that she was not strong in constitution, and that she was endowed with high-strung and sensitive nerves.

Walter Bramber, having heard of the fire, of the threatened arrest of Kate, of her having been taken to the Rectory, hastened to the parsonage in the hope of seeing her. But this Mr. Fielding would not allow. The young man was greatly agitated, grievously distressed. He en-

137

treated to be permitted an interview, but the rector was peremptory in refusing it.

"Remember, all is off between you, at all events for a time. That she likes you, has not ceased to like you, I am convinced. In her present trouble the sight of you would but increase her distress. There is something behind all this—something of mystery, which I do not fathom. Kitty cannot justify herself; not that she is guilty, that neither you nor I credit. There is something that ties her tongue. She is, perhaps, afraid of compromising another, and who that is I do not know."

"I believe," said Walter impetuously, "that this is a wicked conspiracy against Kitty. Mr. Pepperill, to clear himself of the suspicion that he caused the burning down of his stores, painfully laboured to spread the report that Kitty had done it, and done it out of revenge because he refused to allow of my suit. And now he has contrived, by some means or other, to get his rick fired—which is not insured—in such a manner as to make it appear that Kitty, and Kitty alone, could have done it. It is a vile plot to ruin her, and she is innocent as a lamb."

"That she is innocent I am assured," said the rector. "How this last fire has come about I cannot even venture to guess. The material for forming an opinion is not to hand. Till Kitty speaks we probably shall not know, and I do not know what will induce her to speak. Of one thing be confident, Walter: whatever Kitty believes is right, that she will do. I would not urge her to speak, because her sense of duty, her conscience, tells her to be silent. I have that perfect, unshaken trust in her, that I simply leave matters alone, and all I seek is to relieve her of unnecessary trial."

"I am a poor man," said Bramber, "but I will give every penny I have,—I will sell my books, ay, and my violin, to secure the best counsel for her defence, if it comes to that."

"You need not trouble yourself on that score," said Mr. Fielding, with a smile. "Kitty has other friends besides you. There is her aunt, who loves her, and there is her pastor, who watches over her with much care."

Bramber moved in restless unhappiness. The rector saw how wretched the young man was, and he said gently, "Bramber, do you not see that the case is taken almost completely out of our hands?"

"I suppose it is—to some extent."

"Almost entirely. I will not urge Kitty to say what she thinks should be withheld. There is but one thing you and I can do, and that is what I shall advise Kitty, before she goes to bed, that which will be better than any sleeping draught, that which alone will strengthen her to bear what is to come, that will cool the fevered heart, and calm the working brain."

"What is that? I have tried my violin—music will not ease my mind."

"No, it is something else. A prescription I had long ago from a Great Physician: one I have often tried, and never found to fail."

"What is that?"

"Cast all your care upon God, for He careth for you."

Walter clasped the old rector's hand, he could not speak, something rose in his throat. He turned away, and found that the prescription availed.

Before Kitty went to bed that night, the rector sought her. She had been standing for an hour at a window, looking in the direction of the Cellars.

In the few hours that had passed she had become whiter, more sunken under the eyes, more tremulous in her limbs and mouth. It was with her as the rector surmised. Her mind was torn with doubt as to what course she should pursue. If she were to save herself, it must be at the cost of others.

"Mr. Fielding, is it possible to prevent my being brought before the magistrates? that is, can I see my uncle in private here, and induce him to withdraw what he has said?"

"I do not think it is possible."

"I could tell him something which would make him most anxious to hush the matter up."

"Nevertheless, he cannot withdraw. He has made a charge against you. It has gone beyond the stage at which a recall is possible. Remember, Kitty, this is not a mere prosecution for injury done; it is a criminal charge, and your uncle dare not now hold back without making himself guilty of compounding a felony. I am nothing of a lawyer, but I fancy such is the law. Even if your uncle did not take the matter up, Mr. Pooke would be bound to do so. You must make up your mind to that."

"Then something dreadful will happen."

"Kitty," said the rector, "you will have to take my prescription—not mine, but one given by the Greatest of physicians. Unless you do that, you will have no rest for mind or body, no sleep, and you will be worn out before the trial."

"What is that?"

He told her. "The matter, you see, is taken out of your hands. You can do nothing by torturing your brain with thoughts how to avoid this, how to modify that."

"It is so."

"Then cast all your care upon God, for He careth for you. Now go to sleep, and be fresh to-morrow."

The rector left his house and visited the Cellars. The rick was resolved into a huge glowing ember, from which fell avalanches of fiery powder. Above the mass flickered ghost-like blue flames, not in touch with the incandescent heap below.

At the door of the house the rector encountered Pasco Pepperill.

"There—see how I am served by the public!" exclaimed Pasco. "When a misfortune happens, there are always some wanton rascals to do mischief above and beyond what is the main loss."

"What has happened to you now, Mr. Pepperill?" asked the rector.

"Some idle vagabonds have been at my boat again," answered Pasco. "It was so when my stores were burnt— not the same night, but soon after—out of sheer wickedness they cut my old boat adrift, and I lost her. She was carried out by the tide, and never have I heard of her from that day to this."

"Well, and now?"

"And now they've gone and done the same—or worse. Before it was my old boat, and now it's the new one—cut the rope, and away she's gone. It's wickedness. Oh my! You should preach and pray against it. There be such a lot of it in the world—and cost me six guineas did that boat."

"I am very sorry to hear of this additional loss," said the rector.

"I suppose the next thing they will say is, I cut my own boat away and let her go out to sea, because I had insured her. But you may tell everyone, pass'n, that I hadn't insured my boat no more than I had my rick o' straw. Oh dear! the wickedness there is in the world!"

"I wish to see your wife for a moment."

"Zerah's inside, in a fine take-on. She's gone about like a weathercock lately, and can't make enough of Kitty. And now that Kitty is proved to ha' done all these horrible crimes, she's in a bad way, I can assure you."

The rector entered the house and found the poor woman. Her former hardness had given way under the troubles she had undergone; her pride had been broken down beneath the burden of the knowledge that her husband had been guilty of setting fire to his stores for the sake of the insurance money, and of the gnawing suspicion that her brother had died in the flames; that he had been remorselessly

sacrificed by Pasco to conceal his own guilt. And now
that this new conflagration had occurred, and that Kitty
was apparently implicated in it, she was nigh in
despair.

"Mrs. Pepperill," said the rector, "I have come to you
after having dismissed Kitty to rest."

"Rest?" echoed Zerah. "Can she sleep? That is
more than I can."

"Yes; so also will you when you have taken the same
prescription."

"I want no medicine."

"You will take this. You can do nothing for your niece,
can you?"

"Nothing but fret," said Mrs. Pepperill.

"That will not help her. You believe her to be innocent?"
asked the rector.

"I am sure of it."

"Nothing you can say or do will prove it?"

"Nothing; but if I'm called to bear witness, and I must
speak the truth, then what I say may go against her. That
troubles me, terrible. I'm mazed wi' the thought. You
see, I looked, and there was a can'l-end in the lantern
when she took it; and I saw there was none at all when
she brought back the lantern. I don't want to say it, as it
may go against her; but I can't go against my oath and
against the truth."

"Of course not. Speak out what is true."

"And I can't have no rest thinkin', and thinkin', and
frettin' about it all."

"No, Mrs. Pepperill; but you will rest and sleep peacefully after you have taken my prescription—a sovereign one, as many a vexed soul has found—the only one possible in many a case—'Cast all your care upon God, for He careth for you.'"

CHAPTER LII

IN COURT

THE day of the petty sessions at Newton followed closely in the same week, within two days, and whilst excitement was at its height. The court-house was packed, there was hardly standing room; and there was a full bench of magistrates.

Kate was brought in, looking pale; her broad white forehead like ivory, with the dark hair drawn back on either side; the dark eyebrows and long dusky lashes showing conspicuously on account of her pallor; and the lustrous blue eyes, so full of light, alone giving brightness to her face. Though pale, she was composed. She no longer trembled, and her lips were closed and firm.

The transparent purity, the innocent modesty of her bearing and appearance, impressed the court.

She wore a black dress, as she had been accustomed to wear since the fire at the Cellars, in which it was supposed her father had died, but the black was spotted with white, as a sort of concession to the supposition that he might be still alive.

Mr. Fielding was present. He had been courteously

accommodated with a chair within the precincts of the bench; he caught Kitty's eye, and raised his finger, pointing upwards. She understood him, and smiled reassuringly.

Far more anxious than Kitty was Walter Bramber, who had given a holiday to the school, with the rector's consent, and had come into Newton to hear the case. He was not able to master his agitation; his pain to see Kitty in so conspicuous a position, and in such danger, labouring under an accusation which he was certain was unfounded.

Pasco Pepperill was present; he would have to appear in the witness-box. He had sent for his solicitor to conduct the prosecution.

As soon as the case was called, Mr. Squire stood up. He had, he said, a painful task imposed on him, and none felt it more deeply than his client, the plaintiff, who naturally shrank from taking a step of so grave a character, against one who was his wife's niece, young in age, and who had been for many years an inmate of his house, and one for whom hitherto he had entertained an almost fatherly regard. Indeed, so deeply did the plaintiff feel this, that if possible he would have held back altogether, and have borne his loss in silence. But there were attendant circumstances which precluded him from adopting this course. He acted in the matter solely from a sense of duty he owed to himself and to the neighbourhood, and he might add, of humanity towards the unhappy individual placed before the bench under the grave charge of arson.

It was no secret—it could be no secret—that the most serious and damaging reports had been circulated relative to his client in connection with a recent fire at Coombe Cellars, reports most wounding to a man of high integrity and irreproachable character, peculiarly distressing to one of so sensitive and scrupulous a conscience as Mr. Pasco Pepperill, who was churchwarden of his parish, and had served in several important parochial offices, as guardian of the poor, waywarden and overseer, always to the satisfaction of everyone, and had borne, in all his dealings, the character of a straight and upright man.

Mr. Pepperill had formed his own opinions relative to the fire that had occurred on his premises previous to this last, but with them, he, Mr. Squire, would not trouble the bench. Suffice it to say that his view relative to the origin of that fire had impelled him to act with promptitude on the present occasion, not merely to bring to justice the perpetrator of this last atrocious deed, but also to exhibit to the neighbourhood the fact that he had harboured in his house one who was capable of such acts, for which he himself had been most unjustly and cruelly charged by the popular voice.

Moreover, in consideration of the fact that three cases of malicious burning had taken place within a twelvemonth in the parish of Coombe, Mr. Pepperill had thought himself morally bound, in the interest of the public, to prosecute in this last instance, where the criminal had been taken, so to speak, red-handed. And, lastly, he acted in her interest; for he felt, and felt with the most sincere conviction, that it was for the young girl's own good in this world and in the next that a career so badly begun should be checked; and

that by wholesome correction she might be induced to
enter into her own heart and root out from it all malice
and resentfulness which had been allowed, as it would
appear, to harbour there and drive her to the commission
of crime. In conclusion, Mr. Squire hoped to produce
such witnesses—all most reluctant to speak — as would
place the matter clearly before their worships, and leave
them no choice but to refer the case to the Quarter
Sessions. The case being one of felony, they were precluded from dealing with it as in a case of summary
jurisdiction.

Then Mr. Squire proceeded to call Mrs. Zerah Pepperill
into the witness-box. Zerah cast an appealing glance at
Kitty, who acknowledged it gently, with a faint smile.

The solicitor then questioned Mrs. Pepperill.

"You are, I believe, the aunt of the accused?"

"Yes, sir?"

"And you are greatly attached to her?"

"Very greatly.   I have known her from a babe."

"Then we may be quite satisfied that you are most
unwilling to say anything to her prejudice; and that only
an overwhelming sense of duty and responsibility induces
you to give witness—and true witness?"

"Yes, sir."

"Now, Mrs. Pepperill, will you look towards the Bench
and tell their worships, in order, the events of the evening
of the 16th ultimo."

Zerah was silent for a while.

"Do not be afraid; speak out," said the chairman.

"Well, sir," began Zerah, "it was supper—we mostly has our supper at seven, or thereabout. Sometimes we can't be exact. That clock of ours ain't over partic'lar to a minute, and us sets it by the Atmospheric, and the Atmospheric is most irregular of all. Then us took the clock to Mr. Ford, to Newton, to have 'n put to rights, and us paid 'n seven and six, and he sent 'n home worse than he was afore. He used to go, reg'lar, right on end till he runned down, tho' he didn't always keep time exact-ly. But after Mr. Ford took 'n in hand, then he began to stand still, after he wor winded up, out o' pure wickedness; and if you gentlemen would make Mr. Ford pay me back that there seven and six"—

The chairman interrupted her. "Come to the point, please, Mrs. Pepperill."

"Is it the leg o' pork you mean?" asked Zerah. "I'm comin' to her direct-ly. You see, sirs, 'twern't cured proper, not as I likes it, and so the maggots got to the bone. Which do your worships like, gentlemen—rubbin' in the salt dry, or soakin' in brine? I hold to the dry rubbin'—that is, if it be well done; but to have a thing well done you must do it yourself. You can't trust nobody now. And so the maggots"—

"Never mind the maggots, my good woman."

"So I sed to Pasco. Us can't waste thickey leg o' pork; us must eat 'n, and so I'll get 'n out as well as I can, and you go and take plenty o' exercise and work up a cruel strong appetite, and you won't make no count o' there having been maggots in the leg o' pork."

The chairman again intervened, and requested Mr. Squire to extract what was necessary to be known from this good woman by interrogation. If allowed her own course, she would not know where to stop, like the clock before taken in hand by Mr. Ford, and run clean away, as was threatened by the leg of pork.

"Mrs. Pepperill," said Mr. Squire, "you seem to be diffusive in your evidence. However engrossing may be the interest attaching to your clock and leg of pork, still we are not concerned, thank goodness, with either—specially, thank goodness, we are not here to discuss that same leg of pork."

"The leg ought to ha' been turned in the brine twice a day, and her wasn't. If her had been, her'd ha' been famous."

"I rather think, Mrs. Pepperill, this leg of pork is likely to become famous now, as I see a local reporter present, and it will appear in the paper. But this leg is blocking our way; let us lay it on the shelf and proceed, as the French say, to our mutton. Where were you at seven, or, may be, half-past seven, on the evening of the 16th ultimo?"

"I don't think I was nowhere."

"What! nowhere three days ago?"

"That wor the 16th August."

"Well, I said so."

"Beg pardon, sir, you asked for the 16th of Ultimo, and I never heered tell o' that month. It ain't in the calendar."

"Come; on the evening of the 16th last, were you at supper with your husband and others?"

"Yes."

" And those others were "—

" Rose Ash and Noah Flood. They came in "—

"Never mind that. Answer shortly my questions. Where was Kate Quarm?"

"She had her supper, too."

"And when she had done, did she go into the back kitchen to clean up?"

" Yes, sir."

" Was anyone with her then?"

" Yes, sir; Jane Redmore."

"And when Jane Redmore went home, did your niece accompany her?"

"She said she was going with her."

" Did your niece take a lantern?"

" Yes, sir."

"And did you see there was a candle in the lantern?"

" Yes, sir."

" Sufficient to burn for an hour?"

" I don't know that exactly."

" Well, three-quarters of an hour?"

"Perhaps so. I didn't notice exactly how long the candle was."

" Anyhow, it would have burnt for more than a quarter of an hour?"

" Oh yes."

" Or for half an hour?"

" I daresay it would."

"You know it would. Now be careful as to your statements, Mrs. Pepperill. You are quite sure it would have burnt for three-quarters of an hour, if not an hour?"

"Perhaps—I cannot say."

"You can say it would have lasted three-quarters, but are not sure it would last an hour?"

"I suppose so."

"It is not the way of candles, like legs of pork, to run away of themselves, is it?"

"I don't understand you, sir!"

"I mean, that if you put a candle into a lantern, it will remain in the lantern till it is burnt out."

"Unless someone takes it out."

"Exactly! and when the lantern was brought back by Kate Quarm, was the candle there?"

"N—n—o."

"It was not there. It was not burnt out, and it had not run away, eh?"

"I suppose so."

"Then someone must have removed the candle. This is a point, your worships, I wish to establish, and that you should observe. Kate Quarm went out with a lantern in her hand, in which was a piece of candle that would certainly last three-quarters of an hour, if not an entire hour. When she returned, no candle was in the socket. I shall call other witnesses to establish this, and the fact that there were no signs of the candle having melted away; indeed, the lantern is here. Constable, please to produce it. If the Bench will kindly look at it, your worships will perceive that the candle was put in with a piece of brown paper wrapped about it. The paper is still there. The candle is gone. It was taken out. I will call the constable presently to testify that he took charge of the lantern immediately after the event, and that it has not been tampered with since. I now proceed to ask Mrs. Pepperill how long a time Kate Quarm was absent after she went out with Mrs. Jane Redmore. Now, Mrs. Pepperill, pray concentrate your mind and exercise your memory. How long was Kate absent?"

"What—washing up?" asked Zerah.

"No — we have nothing to do with the washing up. After that, when she went out with Jane Redmore."

"I didn't look at the clock."

"About how long?"

"I can't say."

"Do you think it was half an hour?"

"It might be so."

"Or less."

"I really can't tell."

"Then she was absent for half an hour at the outside, possibly."

"I suppose so."

"You may go now. I shall want you again. I proceed to summon Jane Redmore."

This poor woman was in such a nervous condition that she would have fainted, had she not been provided with a chair. Nothing but what was of absolute importance could be drawn from her; which was that Kitty had not accompanied her beyond the gate from the Coombe premises, a distance of hardly three hundred yards.

"This," said the solicitor, "is what I require. I will not trouble this feeble and timorous creature any longer. We have ascertained that the defendant, Kate Quarm, went out with Mrs. Redmore, under the pretext that she was going to accompany her home."

"I do not think this point was established," said the chairman.

"I beg your worship's pardon. You are right. The next witness I shall call will establish the pretext without a doubt. I summon Pasco Pepperill!"

"Stay a moment—what is this noise, this disturbance in the court?" called the chairman. "It is not possible for me or my brother magistrates to hear what is said. Unless the disturbance be allayed instantly, I shall give orders for the court to be cleared."

The requisite stillness ensued.

"Now then, Mr. Pepperill, stand forward, take the book, and such answers," etc.

Again there ensued a movement among the crowd outside the rails—exclamations, mutterings, and heaving and tossing, as though the mass of mankind there densely packed was boiling up from below.

"I insist on order in the court!" called the chairman.

Then Pasco, having kissed the Bible, turned his face to the Bench. He was elate, had spread his breast, and tossed back his head, a self-complacent smirk was on his countenance.

"I have felt it my duty," he said, "to speak—to clear my own self, and to cut short the career of crime of the girl I have regarded as my niece."

Again the agitation among the public; and now through the mob came a man, elbowing his way, till he had forced himself to the front, and stood face to face with Pasco Pepperill.

Pasco, disturbed in his pompous address, turned and saw before him—Jason Quarm !

He put his hand to his head with a gasp, staggered back, and fell senseless to the ground.

CHAPTER LIII

JASON'S STORY

THE court was full of commotion. Pasco Pepperill had fallen, as though struck down by a hammer, and was insensible. He was carried out with difficulty, and with the crowd rushing about him and his bearers, unable to realise what had taken place, anxious to see if he were dead.

He was not dead : a doctor was hastily summoned to the house into which he was taken, and he pronounced the case to be one of apoplexy brought on by sudden and violent emotion.

Meantime, inside the court order was gradually restored.

The chairman made a feeling allusion to the sudden illness which had fallen on the most important witness in the case—which was the less to be wondered at, since the case was one that must deeply move Mr. Pepperill, as he had to appear against a member of his own family.

Then Mr. Pooke, with a mottled face, pushed up to the Bench, and whispered something in the ear of the chairman.

"I beg pardon, I do not understand," said he.

"Sir," said Mr. Pooke, "the real culprit has come to deliver himself up—Jason Quarm, who set fire to the rick, for which his daughter stands here accused wrongfully by the biggest rascal that ever breathed."

"Call Jason Quarm!" said the magistrate.

Jason at once hobbled forward and pushed himself in beside Kate, who was trembling with emotions of the most varied nature. Jason cleared his throat and said—

"I, your worships, I, and none but I, set fire to the rick at Coombe Cellars, and I did it by inadvertence. Please you to remove my daughter from this dock, and hear her presently as witness."

"Let us hear first what you have to say. We cannot discharge her till we know that she is innocent."

"She is innocent, as innocent as the day. May it please your worships to hear what I have to relate. It's a main long story," said Jason.

"What is to the point we will listen to. So you surrender yourself as having fired the rick."

"I did it, your worship. This is how it came about— you may put me on oath if you will."

"Stay a moment. I have to caution you that you are not obliged to say anything, unless you desire to do so; but whatever you say will be taken down in writing, and may be given in evidence against you upon your trial."

"I quite understand that," said Quarm. "If I may be allowed a seat, I shall be obliged. I've got one leg a bit shorter than the other, and it's rayther a trouble for me to stand long, and I've a goodish long tale to tell."

"I again remind you that what you say must be to the point."

"I shan't wander," answered Jason. "But I shall have to begin some way back, and that in March last, when Mr. Pooke's rick was set a-blazin'. That were thought to ha' been the doin' of Roger Redmore, and there was a warrant out agin him, but he wor niver ketched."

"Does this concern the case before the court?"

"Ay, it do—intimate like."

"Very well, then, proceed. We have ordered you to be accommodated with a chair, and your daughter likewise."

"Roger Redmore, he runned away, and the constables never ketched he. My daughter Kitty, her took on terrible over the poor wife as was turned out of house and home by Mr. Pooke, and her persuaded me to let the woman have my cottage, for she and the little ones. I didn't mind, as I was away on the moor busy about Brimpts oak wood, and when I comed back to Coombe, I wor mostly at the Cellars. My sister Zerah, she be that rapscallion Pasco's wife, you understand, your worship."

"Is this really to the point? You are speaking of the fire at Mr. Pooke's, not of that at Mr. Pepperill's."

"One fire hangs on to the other. You'll find that out, gents, when you've heard my tale."

"Proceed, then."

"Well — it seems that Roger Redmore felt mighty grateful because of what Kitty and I had done. I was agent for an insurance company, and I persuaded my brother-in-law to insure in it, but I must say he rather astonished me at the figure at which he insured, and made me a bit uneasy; I hadn't such a terrible high opinion of him as to think he might not be up to tricks."

"What do you mean by tricks?"

"Doin' something to his insured goods that weren't worth much, and gettin' for 'em payment as if they was gold. But, your worship, that you'll say ain't to the point. No more it is—we come to facts, not opinions, don't us? Well, I had been to Brimpts about the oak we was fellin' and barkin', and I wanted to tell my brother-in-law as how I thought we could deal with the dockyard at Portsmouth. So I left the moor and drove down in my conveyance,— which is nothing but a donkey cart and a jackass to draw 'n, —and when I came in the dark o' the evening to my cottage, there I found Roger Redmore in the bosom of his family, so to speak. 'Twas awk'ard for he and awk'ard for me, as there was a warrant out again' him, and so I drove right on and on to the Cellars. I found Pasco there in the house all by hisself, which was coorious. He had sent his wife, my sister Zerah, away somewhere, and Kitty, my daughter, away somewhere else, and he was in a pretty take-on because I turned up unexpected. I didn't quite understand why he was in so poor a temper, and why he should turn me out of the house as he did—and I had got no-where to go to for a night's lodgin'. You see, your worships, I couldn't go home, what wi' all the beds and every hole and corner chockfull o' childer as thick as fleas in a dog's back, not to mention the woman and that chap Roger in hiding, who didn't want to be found. But Pasco, he wouldn't listen to reason, and he was that suspicious and that queer in all his goings - on, that I thought some mischief wor up, and that I'd bide handy and keep an eye on him. Well, gentlemen, when he jostled me out o' the house door, I went to the warehouse, and it wasn't locked, so I stepped in and found the ladder and clambered up that. Thinks I to myself, if Pasco don't mean no wickedness, well, I can sleep here comfortable enough, anyhow. There were plenty o' fleeces — they weren't over clean and sweet, but in such a case one can't be partic'lar. I hadn't been there a terrible long time before I heard the door open and I see'd a light. So I went to the ladder head and looked down, and there sure enough wor Pasco! I watched him awhile to see what May-games he wor up to, and at last I spied what it wor. He were arranging and settling shavings among the coal knobs, so as to make up grand fires, and he was gettin' everything ready to burn down the whole consarn, coals and fleeces and building, and me in it, if I were that jack fool to bide where I was. So I hollered out to he, and let 'n understand who was there, and that I marked his little game. I were on the ladder. He looked towards me, and came at me, and shook the ladder, and shook me down, and I fell on my head, I reckon, and remember nothing more till I came to myself, bound hand and foot in a sack, and throwed a-top of a heap o' coal, that were afire and fizzing out in flame and smoke, and a'most stifled I were, and didn't know 'xactly where I were, whether I'd got to the wrong place down below. I cried out, and I tried to get free, but couldn't move, and then I rolled myself down over fire and coals, and scorched I were a bit; but what'd been the end I cannot tell, if it had not been for Roger Redmore, who broke open the door and came in, and dragged me out of the smoke and smother, and cut the bands and got me out o' the sack, and helped me off to where his missis were, that is to say, my cottage."

Jason paused and looked about him.

"That, I reckon, is the first chapter. Now to go on. When I came there, I thought it all over, and I got Roger to put me in the outhouse, where none of the children might see, and himself he dursn't bide more than the night lest he should be took, but he told Jane to mind me and let me have what I wanted. Well, I turned the matter well over in my head, and I thought as how Pasco were my brother-in-law, and if all came out, I'd bring trouble on Zerah, and on my own child; I'd have to say as how Pasco had fired his own building so as to get the insurance money, and tried to kill me too, 'cause I see'd what he were up to. So I didn't like to do that, and I thought it 'ud be best for all parties if I got out o' the way. I dursn't stir all the day that followed. But at night I got out when I knowed the tide was suitable, and I took the old boat at the Cellars and I made off wi' that, and I rowed out to sea, and rowed along the coast to Torquay, and I landed there, and there I ha' been, unbeknown to the Coombe folk— there or in London. When I'd been a bit to Torquay, I seemed to smell money. I see'd as how a lot o' fortune could be got there by building and making a great place of it for invalids and such folk; and I went up to London to

start a company, and get a building firm to take the matter
up. I've been off and on about this idee, and a fine idee
it is like to turn out—so I reckon. I did hear as how
Pasco, he'd dra'ed twelve hundred pounds out o' the insurance company. Blessed if I knowed 'xactly what I should
do. On the one side, I were agent for the company; on the
other, I were brother-in-law to Pasco, and if I peached on
Pasco, I might just as well ha' stuck a knife into my sister's
heart. And then I owed him something for having reared
my daughter in his house since she wor a baby. And
Pasco and me, us got on famous together about speculations,
and taken in the lump he weren't a bad chap till he began
to look to gettin' money by burning down his warehouse."

Jason stood up, stretched his limbs, sat down again, and
proceeded—after a word of cheer to his daughter, who had
risen and was standing speechless, looking at him with dismayed eyes. She knew that her uncle was false, but Jason
had revealed a depth of wickedness in the man which she
had not conceived to be possible.

She had been satisfied that he had set fire to his magazines
for the sake of the insurance, and she knew that, basely, he
endeavoured to throw the guilt of the act on her. She had
feared that her father had been sacrificed when the warehouse was burned, but had never supposed that her uncle
had done this deliberately.

"Now," continued Quarm, "I reckon I come to the third
chapter. After a bit, I thought I'd come back to Coombe,
but not openly, and see how Kitty were getting along. So I
came unbeknown to everyone, and went to Mrs. Redmore,

and her put me in the same old outhouse as I were in before, and I told her, as she worked at the Cellars, to say nothing about it to Kitty, but find an excuse for getting her out from the house after dark. That is what Jane Redmore did, and I met Kitty at the rick, and us went together behind the rick, so as the light might not be seen from the house whilst we talked. Well, I'd been wi'out my bacca-pipe for some time, and seein' as how Kitty had a light, I told her to open the lantern, and I'd have a bit o' a smoke for comfort. Her opened the lantern door—but Lor'! gentlemen, I han't told you how struck wi' amaze and main glad the little maid was to see her father, whom she had believed to be dead, come to life again, hearty and wi' fine prospects of makin' money out of building speculations to Torquay. But you must imagine all that, your worships; it ain't, as you may say, to the point; but this here little affair o' the pipe and lightin' it is. Well, when she opened the lantern door, I took out the bit end of a candle as was therein, and I put it to my pipe to kindle my 'baccy. She was talkin' and tellin' of me all as had happened, and when her said as how Pasco Pepperill had tried to lay the firing of his warehouse on she, then I were that angry I burnt my fingers wi' the candle-end, not thinking what I were about, and throwed it down right among the straw, and afore I could say Jack Robinson, there was a blaze as no stamping would put out. The first thing Kate did was to run in, and the first thing I did was to tumble into the boat and make off. I didn't know what the consequences might be, and I first thought I'd consider it, and learn what came of it all before I stirred.   If Pasco didn't make a fuss, why, it might pass and no harm come of it; if he made a stir, why, all must come out.   The little maid, I reckon, she would say nothing, because her knowed it was my doing the stack catching alight, and thought she'd bring me into trouble; and then there was that other fire behind; she didn't know what might come if it were examined into, and I made my appearance as one returned from the dead. But I heard of it all.   Jane Redmore sent to tell me.   And now, your worships, I reckon I'm the guilty one of the fire, but it was accident, and she's innocent and may be discharged.   That is my story."

The Bench withdrew for a few minutes.   When the magistrates returned, the buzz of voices in court ceased at once.

"We have decided," said the chairman, "that the case against Kate Quarm be dismissed.   She leaves the court without an imputation against her character.   You, Mr. Jason Quarm, must stand security in yourself and find two others to stand bail for you to reappear before the court when required."

CHAPTER LIV

PASCO PEPPERILL did not recover. The shock had been too great—it had sent the blood rushing to his head, and his consciousness never returned. By midnight he was a dead man.

Now that he was gone, the will—made partly in a moment of scare, partly out of compunction, partly also out of boastfulness—came into force, and Kitty was provided with a small income of her own. The first thing done by her and her aunt, as soon as the will was proved, was to refund to the insurance company the whole of the money paid by them to Pasco on account of the burned stores.

The Cellars belonged now to Zerah for her life. It was not long before an understanding was reached between Walter Bramber and Kitty, the purport of which was that next spring Kitty should cease to be Alone. No inscription, such as the girl had desired, had been cut in the bark of the mulberry tree, and now, were one to be traced there, it would be of a different nature—a legend of two who met and parted, and met again never more to part.

Jason Quarm for once had succeeded in a speculation. The Torquay building society promised to be a prosperous company, and to pay good dividends. Jason was not able to contribute much in capital, but as promoter of the scheme he received certain shares. He was occupied, his mind engrossed in carrying out the plans of the company, in making contracts, in buying materials, in supervising, in altering, in scheming terraces and detached villas, in planting Belle Views and Sea Prospects, and Rosebank Cottages, and Lavender Walks, and Marine Parades, and he could afford no time to be at Coombe.

Zerah was wrapped up in her niece. She could not have loved her more dearly had Kitty been her own child. The hardness in the woman's character gave way; the trouble she had undergone had softened and sweetened a nature really good and kind, but ruffled and soured by adverse circumstances and uncongenial associations. A great change had taken place in the opinion of the public in Coombe-in-Teignhead relative to Kitty. The general feeling was, that she had been hardly treated, in having a crime attributed to her of which she had been guiltless; that if she had been reserved in her manner, it was her way, and all folk were not constituted alike; that if she asked questions, no one was bound to answer them unless he liked, and if he couldn't give the required information. Kitty was quiet—she harmed nobody. She had done Rose Ash a great favour in stepping out of the way when Jan Pooke was inclined to "make a fool of himself wi' her." She was worth three thousand pounds for certain,

and it was said that her father was piling up a fortune in
Torquay.   Coombe Cellars would ultimately be hers, as well
as the little bit of ground about it—or rather, at the back of
it, which was what remained of the farm.   And she had
been grown in Coombe, she had foothold there, and "all
knew the worst o' her, and that weren't so cruel bad."
Finally, and conclusively, Mr. Puddicombe pronounced in
her favour.

So public opinion veered round, and was prepared to
make much of Kate.   The worst that could be spoken
of her was that she had taken up with that schoolmaster
again.   But then, just as Scripture said that the believing
wife might sanctify the heathen husband, so it was reasoned
that the indigenous Kitty might naturalise the foreign
Walter, and that because she belonged to the place, he
might be accepted as a strange plant, given room to root
in at Coombe.

It was very well known that sometimes a stray cat came
to a house from nobody knew where, and meeowed,
entreating to be fed and harboured, and few housewives
would shut it out.   They would take in the stranger, give
it milk and a place by the fire, and domesticate it.   Even
so came this Walter Bramber into Coombe out of space;
whom he had belonged to, and from what sort of
habitation, no one knew.   He asked to be domiciled
in Coombe, and Kitty took him in.   What was allow-
able to a cat was surely not to be refused to a schoolmaster.

If Walter Bramber was afflicted with superior education,

it was probably no more his fault than is water on the brain
in a rickety child.   And if he was a schoolmaster by
profession, perhaps it was not his fault, but his misfortune.
He'd been bred to it by his unfeeling and unnatural parents,
just as in London some boys were brought up to be thieves
and pickpockets.   Mr. Puddicombe, indeed, had taken up
schoolmastering, but that was a different matter; he had
not been reared to anything of the sort, and had adopted
it rather as a pastime than a profession, and had never
allowed it to interfere with his robust and intelligent
pleasures, such as cock-fighting; and Mr. Puddicombe
drank and smoked and swore sometimes, and all that
showed he was a man.   On the whole, Coombe-in-
Teignhead agreed to accept Walter Bramber and Kitty
as his wife, with the proviso that it would kick them over
should they attempt to give themselves airs.

As for the rector, he was radiant with happiness. Now at
last he saw some prospect of making an impression for
good on his parishioners, if not of elevating the existing
generation, of greatly raising the moral and intellectual
tone of that which would follow.   He had striven hard
for years in isolation and with absolutely no success.
Now, with the aid of a peculiarly well-qualified schoolmaster, and with Kitty at that master's side to direct
the girls as Bramber guided the minds of the boys, he
was sanguine of success, not of much that he would see
himself, but of a success in the far future.   Of no profession
can that be said more truly than of that of the pastor,
"One soweth—another reapeth."

"Walter," said he to his schoolmaster, "I was not sent here to blow Sunday soap-bubbles, sometimes iridescent emptiness, sometimes emptiness without the iridescence. Soap-bubbles please for the moment, but they do not satisfy. No father, the gospel says, when asked for bread, will give his children a stone, but a stone has in it substance, whereas a soap-bubble has but emptiness. But the children will not ask for bread unless they be hungry, and will always be pleased to see soap-bubbles sail over their heads. I believe the apostles were sent forth to be the salt of the earth. Their successors are self-satisfied if they be but insipid carbonate of soda. I have striven to feed, not to amuse, but nothing can avail till the hunger come. You find that in the school, I find it in the church. Some Indians chew clay, because they have not bread. Our people have quite a fancy for this stodgy substance; we have to rectify their appetites, so that they may come to desire nourishing diet, and not what is merely stuffing— to seek for instruction, and not amusement. You in your sphere, I in mine, have a similar office, and similar obligations weighing on us, and similar difficulties to encounter. If you seek for popularity, make Puddicombe your model; take the level of the people among whom you are set, and do not stir to cure them of clay-chewing. If you seek to do your duty, then do not expect to have a path of soft herbage to tread, but one of thorns. If I had been indefinite, flowery, hollow in my teaching here, I should have been the most popular man in the parish, and after forty years' ministration would have passed away with a smile of self-satisfaction that I had given no offence to anyone—only to awake in the vast beyond to the startling conviction that I had done no good to anyone!

"Cast your bread on the waters, and you will find it after many days; cast chaff, and it will be blown, washed, rotted away. Many a man in my profession and in yours—we are both teachers—is like the cuckoo-spittle-insect, which throws out a great froth bubble about it. So do some of my profession surround themselves with a copious discharge of words—words without substance. Avoid that in your school, Bramber. Teaching must be definite, or it is trifling, not teaching; and in sacred matters trifling is a guilty desertion of a duty. We are sent to feed, not befool our flocks. Form a clear conception in your mind of what you want to teach, and then impress it sharply, well defined, on the minds given you to act upon. So only will you rear a generation in advance of that to which we belong. But you will get no praise for so doing, save from your own conscience."

Roger Redmore had surrendered to justice, by the advice of Jason, and he had been sentenced to a nominal punishment of two months' imprisonment. Mr. Pooke had readily pleaded for him, had frankly acknowledged that the man had been greatly aggravated, and was perhaps hardly sensible of what he *was* doing.

On leaving prison, Roger was taken, along with his wife, into the service of the Cellars, and gave promise of being a faithful and energetic workman.

The spring arrived in course, and with the warm May air and flowers came the day of Kitty's marriage.

There had been grave discussions among the instrumentalists of the village orchestra previous to the event, as to how it was to be honoured by their performance. In compliment to the ex-schoolmaster, who took a lively interest in the marriage, it was unanimously decided that Puddicombe in F should be performed, if not in its entirety, at all events in part. The "fugg," it was thought, might be omitted, as only a critical and scientific musician could appreciate its merits and disentangle the chaos of sounds. But there was the *largo molto con affettuoso caprizio* at their disposal. As *largo molto* meant, Turn the score upside down, then if the score were not inverted, it would flow in the melody of "Kitty Alone and I." Mr. Puddicombe was approached with the demand whether it were permissible to execute this movement without the *largo molto, i.e.* the inversion of the score. Puddicombe at once assented. That, as he pointed out, was the magnificent brilliancy of the composition, that it could be turned about anyhow, and played right off, and the effect was superb any way. Let them disregard *largo molto* and simply play *con affettuoso caprizio*—which meant, go ahead with the score upright—and there you are.

Accordingly, after the ceremony, when bride and bridegroom issued from the church, the orchestra, which was in readiness, struck up the movement of Puddicombe in F, *con affettuoso caprizio*; and most certainly as it so stood in the score, and so was performed, the air was none other than "The Frog and the Mouse—Crock-a-mydaisy, Kitty alone."

Forward marched the band, playing hautboy, clarionet, first fiddle, second fiddle, the bass labouring along as best he could, tumbling over his viol, throwing out a grunt and a growl when he was able.

The people of Coombe-in-Teignhead were at their doors wishing happiness to the young couple. The children strewed flowers, and every now and then broke out into chorus—

" Crock-a-mydaisy, Kitty alone."

The ploughmen whistled the air and waved their caps. The church bells burst out into clamour and drowned it. The rooks in the elms of the churchyard poured forth volleys of "Caw, caw, caw," introducing a new element into the musical medley.

Through the street went the little procession, headed by children, who danced and sang before the band; then came the musicians, and lastly the married young people. They were on their way to the Cellars, where Zerah was waiting for them, and had brought forth cake and ale in abundance, to feast children, musicians, well-wishers— everyone who would drink the health of bride and bridegroom.

Then, when the regaling was over, and thundering cheers had been given for the schoolmaster, for Kitty, for Zerah— Walter Bramber and Kitty appeared at the door, and half singing, with a smile on his face, to the strain of

"The Frog and the Mouse," Walter thus tendered his thanks—

" Curtsey, Kitty, and say with me—
Neighbours, thanks for company;
On all the world we will shut the door :
In all the world I need nothing more
Than Kitty, my wife, and Kitty Alone,
     Kitty Alone and I."

THE END

MORRISON AND GIBB, PRINTERS, EDINBURGH